# A Gentle Touch

## An Austen Ensemble, Book 3

Corrie Garrett

Kindle Direct Publishing
LOS ANGELES, CALIFORNIA

Corrie Garrett
28 Amherst Rd.
Morgantown, WV 26505
www.corriegarrett. com

Publisher's Note: This is a work of fiction. Names, characters, places, and incidents are a product of the author's imagination. Locales and public names are sometimes used for atmospheric purposes. Any resemblance to actual people, living or dead, or to businesses, companies, events, institutions, or locales is completely coincidental.

Book Layout ©2017 BookDesignTemplates.com

Gentle Touch, A/ Corrie Garrett. -- 1st ed.
ISBN 979-8-88914-002-3

*"After all, life was not made up of moments of exaltation, but of quite ordinary, everyday things."*

—GEORGETTE HEYER, A CIVIL CONTRACT


*To my wonderful husband, Nathan, who gave
me many evenings during quarantine to write
by handling dinner, games,
baths, and bedtime.*

To Lady Catherine de Bourgh,
Rosings Park, Hunsford

*Dear Mother,*

*I am sure you are enjoying your normal good health, but it is customary to start letters with inquiries as to wellness, so please let me know if you are ill.*

*You asked for particulars of our travel plans, and I can now tell you that James and I shall arrive on Thursday, the 28th of November, and stay for two nights to attend the christening of the Collins baby. I am not certain if she has told you, but Charlotte requested that I be a godmother to her new daughter. I believe it is as much a compliment to you as to me, and I accepted, of course. However, Charlotte has chosen to go the traditional route and name two godmothers for her daughter. She asked that I be the one to inform you that the other is Elizabeth Darcy. It is not entirely what I like either, particularly after the hushed but undeniable scandal that occurred with the youngest Bennet girl, but I suppose we must resign ourselves. Recollect that Charlotte was friends with the Bennets long before she was married, and in choosing Elizabeth, she has also gained my cousin Darcy as the godfather. I know you cannot fault that decision.*

*I hope you will allow Mr. and Mrs. Darcy to stay at Rosings for the christening. I completely enter into your sentiments, but since it has been Darcy's custom to stay at Rosings, a deviation would be noted, would it not? We would not want the Hunsford neighborhood to talk about the strangeness of the arrangements and perhaps discompose Charlotte.*

*But enough of unpleasantness. James's young son arrived home last week after a lengthy stay with his maternal grandparents. I have not experienced any sudden burst of maternal instincts, but he is well-enough. He has just turned five years old and tells me he is tall. His nurse has him in hand, and I believe you would find her a solid, honest, and proper woman.*

*James, however, is quite shockingly informal with him. It seems rather plebian to give his son rides on his shoulders or kiss him fondly every night before bed. He will tussle with the boy and even chase about with him and the dogs. I do not have many memories of my father in such a way. I ventured to say something of this to*

*James, but he says London ways will not do in the coun-
try. Did we have London ways at Rosings?*

*James does not act so casually with me, I am thankful
to say. At present, he frequently spends all day out visiting tenants during the slow winter months. I met a few,
but the cold has prevented me accompanying James
again. They seem to be content and tidy, not like the
lazy, indigent families that vex you so in Hunsford.
James says there is not much of that at Middlefinch.*

*He is also overseeing the process of sowing several
fields with sodium nitrate from Chile. I daresay you
wonder at my specificity, but having heard him debate
with himself at length on the merits of many options, I
am far more conversant with farming practice than I
used to be. I told him what you said in your last letter,
that you disapprove of "experimental farmers," but he
merely smiled and said he had no intention of bringing
nitrate to Rosings.*

*I see that marriage is going to involve some conflict.
Since you have been both master and mistress of Rosings for as long as I can remember, I had not realized.*

*James's mother, whom the servants call Lady Be-
atrice, and his uncle, Mr. Obadiah Sutherland, are the
other members of my new household. They call this latter gentleman Obie, a most condescending nickname, I
should think, but he does not seem to object.*

Corrie Garrett

*Overall, I am satisfied with my new home at Middlefinch, and I am slowly learning my duties. I rather thought James's mother might be reluctant to relinquish the rôle of mistress of the house, but she does not seem to have cared for such even before my advent! I have found the house in great need of some refurbishment. Lady Beatrice is a great outdoorswoman and seems to spend her energy in the stables. I hope that when it is warmer, I may join her. At present, I am being careful of my exposure to the unseasonable cold.*

Anne went on to give a detailed account of her health to her mother (an intermittent fever, but otherwise well considering the unusually bitter November).

Anne stopped writing when she realized that little Bernard was peeking at her over the top of the large chair by the fireplace.

"Bernard, you should be in the nursery."

He ducked his head back, but she could still see his small fingers clutching the newly reupholstered brocade arms.

"Bernard."

"It's Barney!" He stuck his head into view at an odd angle, almost upside down.

"How long have you been hiding there?"

"Did I surprise you? I snuck from the hall and crawled under the piano. Then I crouched behind the settee, and then into the chair!"

"Does Nurse know where you are?"

"Today is Nurse's day off."

Anne frowned. "Then who is minding you?"

He looked a little self-conscious. "What are you writing?" he asked quickly.

"A letter to my mother."

"My mamma is dead," he declared.

"Yes, I know."

He sidled over to the writing desk. His brown hair was wavy and rather long, and his shirt was tucked into plain breeches under a pea-green jacket. "You're my new mamma."

"Yes."

"Do you like me?" he asked. "Nurse keeps asking me if *I* like *you,* but I do not know if *you* like *me.*"

Anne blinked. "I do not *dislike* you," she said scrupulously. "But I do not know you well enough to like you. I like very few people."

The boy nodded thoughtfully. "Fair enough."

"That is a vulgar way to respond to an adult."

"Why?"

"It is... careless."

A rapid set of footsteps was heard descending the stairs.

"Now I'm in the basket!" Barney yelped. He shot off toward the double doors that led to the Great Hall and the front entrance to the house.

Nurse appeared at the door, much flushed. "I beg your pardon, ma'am," she said stiffly. "Betty the housemaid was to watch him on my day off, but she was called away and forgot to tell me."

"Perhaps another person would be better suited to watch him next time." Anne turned back to her letter. "You're free to go after him."

Nurse lingered in the doorway for a moment.

"Is there aught else?" Anne asked.

"I— No, ma'am."

She departed and Anne began a letter to Charlotte, but she only managed a few sentences before she was interrupted again, this time by her husband.

"Hullo, Anne." He placed a hand on her shoulder, glancing at the thick cream paper on the escritoire, a fine French-made writing desk. "Penning a letter to your friend? That's good."

Anne tensed when he touched her like this. She did not mean to. He was her husband and had the right to touch her, but it still felt strange and unnatural to have a man, or anyone, casually put his hand on her.

"You could ask her to come for a visit, though I daresay she will want to wait until it warms up," he suggested.

"We will see her at the christening next week."

"Yes, of course. Do you like infants?" he asked. His hand was still on her shoulder, not at all harsh or even heavy, but there.

"I have no experience of them. I always thought I should be too ill to have children of my own and took no interest in them."

"Hm." His hand finally left her shoulder, which she was glad of, except that now she felt suddenly cold. She shivered.

James went over to the fire and poked it with the heavy, wrought-iron tongs until it was flickering high again.

"Would you ring for tea?" He rested his foot on the brass fender. "It is a little early, but I am famished."

"Of course." She turned over her letter and put the quill in the standish. She pulled the rope, and when the maid came, relayed the order.

James settled into a chair near the fire and idly spun the queen of a chess set, which rested on a highly polished, checkered wooden table. "Now that we are settled here in Middlefinch and Barney is back, we must find a few activities to pass these quiet winter days."

Anne sat in the adjoining chair. "I never learnt chess; my mother prefers whist or card games of that sort."

"But you cannot play that with two people," he protested.

"True. What activities did you do with your first wife?"

James looked toward the window which had a view on the snowy orchards and rear garden of Middlefinch. Anne followed his gaze. The trees were pruned back, looking lifeless and bare. The roses and other delicate flowers along the walk were trimmed and tied up. They looked like tiny old women crouching in rows in the snow.

On the west side of the house, the unseasonable snow was nearly pristine. On the east side, however, there were muddy tracks from the hothouse vegetable garden to the kitchens, and wheelbarrow tracks to and from the stables.

"In the winter Milly and I played chess," James said presently, "or cribbage, or backgammon. Sometimes she would read aloud, or I would read aloud to her. Of an evening, she would play or sew or embroider until we retired to be cozy. But in the summer, there were more options: walking, riding, paying visits..." He trailed off. "What did you do to amuse yourself at Rosings?"

Anne rubbed her cold fingers. "In good weather, I often rode out in my little carriage. I cannot read for long periods myself, as it makes my head ache, but my companion would read to me." That was true, as far as it went, but even more often in the winter months, Anne found herself sitting for hours watching the fire burn while nursing an aching body or head cold, wheezing distressingly. Then she would eat a nuncheon with her mother, who would share community news with her. Anne usually needed to lie down before dinner, and after dinner she retired early to bed and waited numbly for the next day.

"I would not mind learning chess or cribbage or backgammon," Anne said.

James smiled. "That's the spirit."

As James explained the rules of the game and the names of the chess pieces, he couldn't help wondering why his expectations of Anne had been off the mark. He had known Anne was invalidish for many years and was only recently feeling stronger. He had known she had an autocratic mother who would inevitably think Middlefinch an extension of her domain. He had known that Anne was slightly unusual for a woman, pleasingly blunt and straightforward.

But he had, perhaps naively, believed that Anne would be a trifle more cheerful as a happily married lady. He was convinced that women responded to affection, and so he had assumed that Anne, though not sentimental and not the sort to fancy herself in love, would be forthright and friendly and... well, happier.

Instead, she seemed rather more silent and austere than she had done during his summer visit or their trip to Hertfordshire.

James wasn't one to quibble over preferences, but he was a genial man and liked to be surrounded by cheerful faces. He particularly wanted those dependent on him to be content. It troubled him to come home and find Anne sitting silent, solitary, and solemn before the fire. His mother, whom he discreetly asked, said that Anne did this often and for hours at a time.

James, himself happiest when occupied, could not understand it. Of course, everyone knew ladies needed less stimulation than men, but on the other hand, his mother enjoyed her horses and hounds as much as any gentleman.

At first James feared Anne was dissatisfied or home-sick, but she flatly denied either. She seemed to expect and perhaps even prefer such days, days that to him seemed unutterably dull and empty.

When he joined her every evening, she was scarcely more animated. At first James did not notice, being, well, not a *gabster,* but a talkative man. And there was much to tell Anne about her new home and its environs. But as those topics began to fall away, James noticed how little conversation Anne introduced. Again, prefer-ences were preferences—his mother and uncle had taught him that!—but he could not quite envision the evenings of the next several decades going by in such a one-sided way.

"I will move first," James said, bumping a pawn two spaces forward. "Remember that they only attack diagonally, and after their first bold move can only advance one space at a time."

Anne followed suit and they took turns, with James pointing out various traps or opportunities for her pieces.

She did not look precisely happy to be playing, but she was intent and that was better than the dreadful blankness she was prone to.

When she tried to move her king into check, he put his hand over hers. "Not there, take note of my knight's position."

Her hand was cold, and her thin knuckles felt like pebbles under his hand.

She made a better move, but he still put her in checkmate not too many plays later.

"Good for a first game," James declared.

Anne began setting the pieces back into their places. "Let us play again."

"You needn't."

"I want to. I understand the moves now."

James grinned. "Pluck to the backbone. At this rate, you'll be a formidable foe by spring."

{ 2 }

ANNE WOKE ACHING, TIRED, and slightly fever-ish the next morning. A heavy rain made a dull, pervasive noise that muted the normal sounds of the household. Where the housemaid had drawn back the drapes, thick ribbons of water traced patterns down the glass. The snow was gone and the drive which curved in front of the house was muddy and rutted. James really ought to have gravel put down, as her mother had suggested.

The park beyond was a mix of winter-bare turf and a few flickers of lingering green leaves in the trees that lined the drive and encroached from the woods. Those glimpses of green were few and far between, surrounded by the brownish gray of bare branches and shrubs.

Anne pressed her forehead to the cold windowpane, but it did not help the ache there and caused a violent shiver. She used to feel this uncomfortable every day, but she had grown distressingly accustomed to pain-free mornings, making this particularly unpleasant. She rang for her abigail, Susan, who brought warm water for washing and helped her to dress. Anne groaned quietly as she lifted her arms over her head while Susan tugged the gown into place. Susan was a good girl, but not a companion or friend.

Anne had dismissed Mrs. Jenkinson before the wedding. The lady had been with her for years, but Anne could not forget the piece of a letter she had accidentally seen, the letter in which Mrs. Jenkinson shared how little love she had for Anne.

Perhaps Anne should speak to James about hiring a new companion. She did not need one for propriety's sake any longer, but if she was to have a sickly winter...

Susan draped a warm merino shawl around Anne. "It's colder here than at home, and no mistake. Timothy, one of the grooms, says as how we are not far from Rosings, so I must be imagining it, but I say anything over five miles is far. You cannot walk it! The servants all say Old Joseph knows the weather—"

"Yes, Susan, that will do," Anne said, dismissing the maid.

In the dining room, which thankfully was on the same floor as her bedroom and therefore did not require use of the stairs, Anne joined James's mother, Lady Beatrice. The room was warmly decorated in shades of tan, gold, and white, but when Anne had complimented Lady

Beatrice on this, she had been informed that James's late wife, Millicent, was responsible for the décor.

An empty plate lay before Lady Beatrice, only a few bites and crumbs of toast remaining. She was polishing off a cup of tea. Lady Beatrice was a large, squarely built woman, whose arms were round and strong, and whose hands were distressingly red. Her face was also a square, not plain or ugly, but not distinguished, raised only above the average by her richly-colored auburn hair which she often wore wrapped around her head in a sort of coronet, and which showed only the faintest hints of gray at the temples.

"Good morning," Anne said. She did not feel well enough to eat but poured herself a cup of tea.

"It is probably cold," Lady Beatrice told her, not unkindly. "You should ring for a fresh pot."

"Very well." Anne quietly did so.

"I'm going out to help Old Joseph in the stables this morning. He says there's a mass forming on Morning Song's knee, and I want to examine it. Possibly a warm poultice will help if it's weeping."

Lady Beatrice had yet to *not* go to the stables of a morning, excepting Sundays. Anne sipped her tea; it was indeed cold. "My groom at home made one with bran and clay and several herbs—it worked well."

Lady Beatrice shook her head decidedly. "If I was to take a new recipe to Old Joseph...! He would sulk for days."

"My mother says the feelings of servants are often mere ploys. A firm hand—"

Lady Beatrice put down her teacup a trifle quickly. "I daresay; but she does not know Old Joseph. He has been at Middlefinch since the Dark Ages, more or less. I shouldn't want to hurt his feelings and he does know the devil—excuse me, the *deuce*—of a lot about horses." She rose. "If you care to come to the stables this morning, I should be happy to introduce you to our beauties."

"No, I should not expose myself to the cold." Anne received the new teapot from the footman and missed Lady Beatrice's look, which flickered between relief and something akin to contempt as she took her leave.

Anne genuinely looked forward to becoming acquainted with the Middlefinch stock. She hoped very much that, when it was warmer, she might begin to ride or drive out as she had done at home. Perhaps James would even take her to the races at Ashford or Lingfield; his horses often raced in those two nearby racecourses and were often well-placed, she was told.

But she knew it would be the height of folly to go out in the damp cold of a snowy November day. She was already more worn down than she would like, and when she caught a cough in November it tended to last until

February, and that was if it did not turn to outright pneumonia.

She was contemplating a second cup of tea when James's uncle poked his head in. He had height but none of Lady Beatrice's girth, being a rather thin man with a concave chest. His face was a rectangle rather than a square. He held a small notebook in his hand, into which he was always scribbling stories. Anne was nervous around him.

He entered and looked blankly at the table, then at her. "Do you find that ghosts are still a source of uncanny thrill, or has their mystery worn out? Is your generation too scientific to believe in the pure specter any longer?"

"I do not believe in ghosts," Anne offered.

"No, I feared not," he said gloomily. He sat heavily across from her. He put the notebook into his pocket and idly picked up a muffin with his long, knobby fingers. "What does frighten you? Please tell me. Whenever I put pen to paper, it is the ghouls and headless horsemen and white ladies who speak to me, but their hoarse voices are become so commonplace I can hardly forbear offering them tea."

Anne sipped her cold tea uncomfortably. This Mr. Sutherland was not actually an uncle of the family, but he was a cousin of James's father and had long held that honorific. He was furthermore a writer of novels and plays, and as such, a completely unknown quantity to Anne. He also often forgot her name, which was rather off-putting. Today, at least, he seemed to know who she was.

"Any fears will do," he repeated presently. "What puts you in a chill of dread? Perhaps the jointed legs of the arachnid or the white bones in a charnel house? The rot of a dead body, or the nightmare of drowning—"

"Suffocation," Anne blurted, mostly to make him stop. "I would not like to die for lack of breath. I know it is not the worst fate, not like a pyre or plague, but it seems to me quite horrible."

He got out his notebook and a rather grubby pencil. "Oh, yes? Yes, that is a thought," he muttered. "There is the breath of life. Genesis. And breath is often associated with soul. Yes, suffocation is excellent. Suffocation of the soul, even? Hm."

"I do not know."

He suddenly looked intently at her. "What think you of automatons?"

Anne was thankful to pour the hot tea that the butler, Bronson, delivered. "I am sure I don't know. The idea of a lifeless machine that mimics the human body does not horrify or excite me; it merely seems foolish. James likes technological advancements, perhaps you should ask him."

Obie bit his pencil. "Yes. Yes, he does like new inventions."

Anne thought Obie had forgotten about her, but then his eyes cleared again, and he pointed his pencil in her direction. "Very helpful. What do you say to an automaton that goes at night to the master's room, perhaps crawling up the stairs on unfinished copper limbs, slowly sucking the breath of life and soul out of him?"

Anne grimaced. "Now you *have* made it horrifying."

"Yes, it is, isn't it?" he said delightedly. "Quite the most terrible idea I have had for some time. And perhaps as the automaton does so, she grows more lifelike, yes, more animated."

"She?"

"And when the man realizes what is happening— shall I have a tragic young wife discover it to her lasting mental horror? Or shall it *be* the young wife to *his* lasting mental horror? Regardless, he must choose between his life's work and his own life! But he shall fight back, oh certainly, but probably too late. This is extremely morbid, thank you."

Anne suppressed a shudder. "Why would you write such a thing, sir? Surely it is as unprofitable to meditate upon in composition as it should be upon reading."

"Unprofitable?" He looked blank, but hardly chastened, as if he did not know the word.

Anne recollected that it was not her place to chasten him, being that he was of the older generation and of her husband's family.

"I apologize. I hope you..." Anne was at a loss. It was not in her nature to wish people joy of a task, nor had she ever been trained to do so. Joy was largely irrelevant, was it not? To fulfill duties, to exercise just authority, to improve oneself—were those not the hallmarks of a proper life?

"I shall enjoy myself prodigiously," he assured her. "I must make some sketches. Do you draw?"

"No, not particularly."

"Ah, of course not. Neither do I, but I shall muddle through."

He soon left her, taking another muffin in hand, and a third in his pocket. What a strange man!

Anne retired to the drawing room where she generally spent the morning. She had written to her mother and Charlotte yesterday, and she did not have any other correspondence to answer at present. She sat herself near the fire.

She was still sitting there as various servants passed through the house on their morning chores and errands. She was unaware of the continued whispers about the strange and still mistress of the house.

How long she sat thus Anne was not certain, it could have been half an hour or three. But presently—

becoming uncomfortable with the vision of misshapen metallic men that currently occupied her mind—Anne recollected the chess board. She sat herself before it and rubbed a knight in her hand, finding the satin finish rather satisfying. She reviewed the various moves in her head, and then she began a tentative game, playing both the black and white pieces.

Anne looked guiltily at the doors several times. It seemed decadent and—and frivolous to spend a morning playing a game. Sitting quietly before the fire, while not productive, seemed at least to be lady-like. This felt more indulgent.

But with Mr. Obie Sutherland upstairs writing his gruesome stories, Lady Beatrice in the stables with her beloved horses, it did not seem so wrong. And her husband *wished* her to learn chess, so perhaps she could salve her conscience in that way.

WHEN THE HOUSEKEEPER, Mrs. Gridley, rapped lightly at the door, asking to speak with her, Anne was conscious of a guilty start. She smoothed her skirt and began replacing the pieces to their starting positions, as if she was just idly tidying them up.

"I know we've already gone over the weekly menu, ma'am, but Cook is perturbed as can be, for John couldn't find fresh oysters at the market a'tall."

"Oh. Perhaps Lady Beatrice..." But Anne knew as soon as she said it that she had erred. The briefest expression of disdain crossed the housekeeper's face. *Anne* was now the mistress of Middlefinch. It was shirking her duty to send these matters to Lady Beatrice. And that lady, whom Anne had thought might resent her, was rarely to be found in the house at all. "I do not mind if the oysters in caper sauce are replaced by another dish. I am sure the cook can decide what would be appropriate."

"Well, he's right dithered to do so, ma'am. I think you must speak with him. High-strung, you know."

Anne followed Mrs. Gridley through the great hall, down the servant's hall, past the back stairs, and into the kitchens. Her first thought was that it was delightfully warm in here, and her second thought was that surely the little boy sitting under the large wooden table was Barney?

But she was distracted by the cook. She'd met him before, when she was introduced to the staff, but had not yet invaded his kitchen. Normally the housekeeper took Anne's orders on the first day of the week and relayed them to him, and generally those orders merely consisted of agreeing to the menu he provided.

"A thousand apologies, madam." He bowed. "You should not have troubled yourself to come to Luc's kitchen."

Anne found that rather inconsistent, as she had essentially been summoned to him, but she let it pass. "I understand there are no fresh oysters."

"Yes, ma'am. It is undoubtedly the fault of the tides; they are not regular when the snow comes early and that delays the fishermen, but what is Luc to do without oysters?"

"I do not have a strong preference," Anne said. "Perhaps partridge or even chicken—"

"With a beef ragout?" he cried. He eyed her gown and waved at it approvingly. "Would you put on a fuchsia cloak with your ensemble? Purple or teal? Of course not. Clearly sable or cherry, yes?"

Anne smiled in spite of herself. "Why, yes. I generally wear a sable with this—"

"*Bien sûr!* Of course. *Dites-moi.* I must complement the beef. If it were a feast or public day, it would be different, but it is not."

Anne spread a hand. "What would you suggest?"

"To take the place of oysters *mignonette*?" He tapped his neatly trimmed mustache. "It is not merely to spin in the larder and point to the first item you see. Perhaps a *bouillabaisse* or a white soup..." He argued with himself for some minutes, but eventually settled on a dish. Anne found herself agreeing that it was a most difficult task, and upon receiving this encouragement, he spent some minutes explaining the particular preferences of Lady Beatrice, her son, and Mr. Obadiah, as well as the difficulties of using the rather alarmingly modern stove that James had caused to be installed.

"Always the latest in everything, that is what he likes," the cook said, obviously torn between pride and criticism of his master. "He likes it no matter how difficult it may make my life, but I do not complain! *Au courant* is the master, yes, always the most fashionable, but not in clothes, in the machinery."

Anne noticed that Barney had gone very still under the table since she arrived. He could not very well crawl out and escape into the house without treading nearly upon her feet, so he seemed to be hoping to avoid detection. A pile of spillikins lay just in front of him. Occasionally his play instinct got the better of him, or perhaps his patience was wearing thin, and he would stealthily remove a stick from the pile that comprised his game. Anne felt a strange urge to smile, which was clearly inappropriate since he must be playing truant again.

She leaned over slightly and made eye contact with him. "Bernard."

"It's *Barney.*" With a sigh, he collected the ivory sticks of his game and slid them with practiced ease into the pocket of his tidy jacket. "I'm coming. I knew you would send me back up to the nursery."

"I think perhaps I shall escort you," Anne said. "You do seem to escape with some frequency."

Anne had to pause on the stairs to breathe, as climbing up two tall flights of stairs, from the kitchens to the nursery, was a little taxing. Barney unexpectedly took her hand. "Are you sick? Nurse makes me drink broth when I'm sick and I don't mind that, but I don't like the nasty, sticky medicine she gives me."

"No, I am not ill. Not yet."

"Not yet?"

"I tend to be ill every winter."

He looked horrified but impressed. "Every winter of your life? But that would be so many! F-fifty-six!"

Anne again felt the urge to laugh. "No, I am only twenty-three."

Barney continued to hold her hand as they went up the stairs. Anne did not feel right shaking him off, so she allowed it. There was something very strange about having a small, pudgy hand tucked into her own. Something almost... nostalgic, though she did not remember holding her mother or father's hand as a child.

Barney was fair child with pale skin and curly straw-colored hair, which Anne assumed must come from his mother's side. He cheeks grew flushed with any excitement, and he would probable freckle as he grew older. His eyes were a grayish-blue, however, very much like James's.

The nursery was on the top floor of the house, along with his nurse's room, the guest rooms, and the suite allotted to Mr. Obadiah. The nursery was as well fitted out as any nursery Anne could imagine for a boy. A plump rocking horse stood at attention near the window, a wooden puzzle with oddly shaped pieces lay scattered on a braided rug, and shelves of books lined either side of the fireplace. A small, intricate steam engine and cars occupied the farther corner of the room. There was even a very small table, clearly made for a child, with two tiny matching chairs. Nearer to the fire sat two larger, finely upholstered chairs. In one of these, Nurse was sleeping. An open book lay in her lap, one limp hand holding it in place.

Anne cleared her throat and Barney looked scandalized.

"She's *sleeping*," he said.

"Yes, I know, but she ought not to sleep while on duty."

"I know. And I *can* wake anyone, because I am the master and they are my servants." He kicked a toe into the thick carpet. "But then, Nurse is probably tired because of me, and Father says we must be kind to our servants. Besides, when she wakes up, she will make me do *lessons*."

"Ah, I see."

"She probably *deserves* a good rest..."

But their voices had wakened Nurse, who bounced unsteadily to her feet. She was already pale and looked more so when she saw Anne standing there with Barney. She was no fool and immediately realized that she must have been asleep for some time.

"I beg your pardon, ma'am. I hope Barney hasn't been plaguing you."

Anne looked at Barney, his small hand still in hers. For the first time, a dark, unused corner of Anne's mind was illuminated, a spark of empathy. "No, he was not plaguing me. In fact, he was quite minding his own business. I suppose you might say I am plaguing him."

Nurse's face wavered near a smile, but uncertainly. "Yes, ma'am. I do apologize, ma'am." She hesitated. "Would you like to inspect Master Barney's rooms while you are here?"

"My puzzle," Barney said. "You can help me with my dissected puzzle. Nurse says it is crafted to addle the brain."

She blushed. "It is too difficult for me, ma'am. And if Master Barney so much as bumps it, it destroys hours of work."

Barney tugged Anne over to the rug. Anne disengaged her hand gently, not willing to be pulled to the floor.

"You must bring all the pieces to this little table," Anne said presently. "It will never work on a tufty rug. Is it a map?" Anne had had a rather beautiful dissected map of Europe that she enjoyed greatly as a child. In fact, perhaps she could ask her mother to send it to Middlefinch, if it had not been thrown out.

Barney brought handfuls of the small pieces to the table, returning for more. "No, I think it is something botanical. Nurse says there is ever so much Latin on it."

He brought back more while Anne seated herself on a low chair. "Your father loves farming, so I daresay you are right. Make sure you get every piece," Anne reminded him. "I have no intention of working for hours only to have it all be for naught."

Barney grinned while retrieving a piece that had inexplicably worked its way under the rocking horse.

"Excellent," said Anne. "It seems to me we ought to spread out the pieces and turn them all upright."

Barney fiddled with two pieces, turning the left one this way and that. "That will take an awful long time."

"You do not have to, I suppose," Anne said, somewhat sternly. "But you did ask for my help."

Barney sat up. "Yes, 'm. I did. Let's do what you said."

James came up to the nursery to say hullo to Barney before finding Anne for a midafternoon luncheon. He was more than a little surprised to find Anne in the nursery as well. She sat on one of the tiny chairs and was thoughtfully fitting a piece of the botanical puzzle he'd bought Barney for his birthday into a hole.

"Now, do you stop hopping all about like a kangaroo," she said, "or you shall bump the table again."

The pieces were cut into separate shapes, but mainly with smooth edges. It was very easy to disarrange.

"Five pieces, five pieces!" Barney sang. "Just as I am five."

"Then you shall do the last five. I am expecting you to be very careful." While Barney placed the pieces, nearly holding his breath, Anne closed her eyes and gently pressed on them with a wince. James frowned. Had she given herself a headache with such close work?

But she opened her eyes and smiled with heavy lids at Barney as he finished the puzzle.

"And your father has come just in time to see it," Anne said.

James admired their work and read some of the names for Barney. "Over here, this tree is the *citrus reticulata,* the tangerine orange that we have in your mother's *lemongerie.* Imported from China."

Barney clutched his stomach. "Talking about oranges makes me *starving.*"

"You're not starving," James said, ruffling his hair, "but you are no doubt ready for your meal." He held out his hand to Anne, who wobbled a little as she stood from the small chair. "And we will go have our luncheon as well."

When he and Anne were seated in the dining room, where they were joined by his mother, Anne again made that motion of distress, pressing her eyes to relieve the pain in her head.

"I fear you have overtired your eyes," James said. "It was kind of you to play with Barney, but you must not feel bound to stay in the nursery longer than you like."

Anne had put very little on her plate. "I did not feel imposed upon; I enjoyed completing the task with him. My head was already aching this morning, and it was...agreeable to be distracted."

"Yes, play with the boy," Lady Beatrice agreed. "Far better to be up and doing than otherwise. I am sure if I sit before the fire too long, I begin to have the megrims no matter how hale and healthy I may be."

James helped himself to a large plate of mutton and potatoes. "You must let me know if there is anything I can do when you feel low. Perhaps you had better have brought your companion to Middlefinch. She could at least read to you, keep you company... distract you from any discomfort, as you say."

Anne was silent rather longer than the comment seemed to occasion. "Mrs. Jenkinson was ready to move on. I had considered the possibility of a new companion, but...I find the thought of paying a stranger for a simulation of friendship dispiriting."

"That is a fair point," James admitted. "In fact, I have sometimes wondered at all these companions for ill ladies, young ladies, widows, and so on. The position is often filled by a poor relation who is treated like a drudge, and where is the fellowship in such company as that? With the young ladies, it is a dragon hired to safeguard her reputation, a cross between a warden and an upper servant, which I cannot imagine leads to much affection. The simulation of friendship for a salary, as you say."

Lady Beatrice wiped her mouth. "That is a great piece of nonsense. If a lady needs attending, how else should she go about it? Friends a lady may have, but not many friends are in the position to leave all and attend to her. An employee is what is needed, and a salary is necessary. Some are born to more, and some to less, and as long as there is mutual understanding, all is well. There is no reason the relationship may not also be *friendly,* but look for true friends elsewhere."

"You are no doubt correct, ma'am," Anne said quietly. "I suppose for quite a long while I did not have many outside acquaintance. I mistakenly looked to my companion for such friendship, giving me an irrational distaste of them."

James's cheerful soul felt a twinge. "I regret that you haven't been able to make any friends here yet; this cursed early winter is to blame. But this spring we shall go to London for the Season, as I promised. And in the meantime, you have myself and my mother, and Obie, of course. You are not quite alone."

"No, not at all," Anne said. "I did not mean to complain; I am not lonely."

"Not lonely," Obie repeated.

"And here is a thought," James said, pleased with himself. "What if you were to ask one of Mrs. Collins's sisters to be a companion to you? She is a good friend, yes? And you met her family in Hertfordshire. I am sure one of them should suit."

Anne tilted her head. "I had not thought of that. It is certainly an idea."

James smiled, feeling the matter was all but settled. The twinge abated.

Anne felt rather better after lying down for the afternoon and hesitantly joined James in his study when he waved her in.

"Hullo, my dear. I am just copying the last notes from the turnip-planting of the home farm. I think next year I might move sowing a week earlier." He was transcribing from a small pocketbook to a ledger.

Anne did not have much to venture on this topic, and idly spun the globe on its stand. It was a fine model. Presently James put away his pocketbook. "We received the christening gift from London today."

"Oh, yes?"

He went over to a side table and picked up a tidy parcel wrapped with rich, shiny paper and a double loop of string. He carefully unwrapped the whole, opening the box to show her two fine silver cups, gourd-shaped and double-handled. "This is what you ordered?"

Anne took one and smoothed her thumb over the cold, shiny face. The whole was embossed with vines and flowers. The metal was thin but very fine. "Yes, I am quite satisfied. Very fine work."

"What sort of cup is that?" James asked. "I believe my mother has something similar on a shelf in her sitting room."

"A caudle cup. Traditionally, it is for the new mother as she recovers, to drink the restorative caudle, which was usually made of wine, gruel, eggs, and sugar. Most ladies do not use them anymore, or drink such stuff, but many ladies treasure the cups as keepsakes or even heirlooms."

"Well, they are quite pretty and will make a fine set upon a shelf. I hope the babe likes them."

"I do not know the baby," Anne said, replacing the cup. "But I do believe Mrs. Collins will be pleased."

"An incontrovertible argument. We must make the baby's acquaintance."

"Are you laughing at me?"

"No, not at all. I think you are very right! What is more, the mother is the one who might need some encouragement while the babe is the one lavished with attention. By the by, did you write your mother about Mr. and Mrs. Darcy?"

"I urged her to receive them, as you suggested, though I am still not sure it was necessary. My mother deplores anything that causes talk in the neighborhood."

James carefully repacked the gift, wrapping it up and retying the string. "I hope you are correct. They seem an unexceptionable couple. I hate to see families angry and feuding over such things."

Anne felt rather defensive. "My mother is not angry."

James gave a crack of laughter, but then cleared his throat. "I beg your pardon, my dear, but she was livid about the connection. She made no secret of it."

"But you make it sound as if she were merely indulging spleen. My mother felt wrongly used by Elizabeth, who did, I must agree, flirt shamelessly with my cousin."

"But clearly he is besotted with her and she with him; can you blame them for that?" James sat on the bench beside Anne and took her hand. "I have never ventured to speak of it, but I could not help but know that your mother intended you for Mr. Darcy. I do not know what your feelings were, but I hope it was not a shock of long duration."

Anne felt again that uncomfortable frisson when he took her hand, but there was no denying the pleasant warmth of his fingers. "I do not mind you speaking of it; I believe it was generally known."

"Yes, unfortunately it was. Friend of mine in London wrote recently that it made a bit of stir—Darcy marrying elsewhere and disobliging his family, that is. The business with Lizzy's baby sister didn't help any. But such things blow over quickly. I only wondered how you were affected."

"You needn't. I felt surprisingly little when I learned he had offered for her."

"Well, good. You know how much I prefer to discuss these *unsaid* things. I am, on my own behalf, quite glad that things have fallen out as they have. You are much better here with me; I hope eventually you will feel the same."

"Yes, I do," Anne realized. She had never juxtaposed the two situations so clearly before. When Anne thought of what marriage to Darcy would truly have meant, now that she was a matron of a whole month, her life seemed better as it was.

"I do not regret him," Anne explained. "Darcy is a gentleman, but...he rarely says what he is thinking."

James laughed, releasing her hand. "As opposed to your dear husband, who is a sad rattle." He reached over and spun the globe again. "Fancy a game of chess before dinner?"

"Certainly." She still rankled a bit at his criticism of her mother, but he had in some manner diffused the conflict.

James's mother and uncle joined them before long, dressed for supper. Obie pulled up a chair and watched the chess game, leaning dreamily on one hand. "You are no match for him, Mary, his queen already has spared both your knights."

"My name is not Mary, it's Anne," she reminded him. "And he did not spare them..." But she saw that Obie was correct. James could have taken both her knights in the last two moves. How irritating that even strange, absent-minded Obie was better at this game than she.

"You should have your automaton play chess," Anne said, a little sharply. "A detailed anecdote might make the rest more believable."

"Yes," Obie agreed reaching for his notebook. "Definitely chess. The sort of thing an automaton would like."

James raised his brows. "Has Obie been reading his work to you? He will rarely tell me anything."

Obie smiled seraphically. "Mary helped me find a plot for a new story."

"I am not Mary," Anne repeated.

Obie's face fell a trifle and he looked away uncomfortably.

Later, when they made their way to dinner, Lady Beatrice put her hand on Anne's arm. "I understand Obie may be irksome to a stranger, but he is more sensitive than he lets on. I believe, if it should not greatly trouble you, there is no harm in letting him think of you as Mary when he is confused. He often has a jumble of names in his head from his silly ghost stories."

"But that is not my name."

"No, and sometimes firm correction is needed, but other times... May I suggest a gentle touch will do?"

Anne couldn't help but think what her mother would say to such a weak-willed philosophy; how disastrous it would be in both general and particular circumstances. "That is not how I was raised."

"No," Lady Beatrice sighed. "So I've gathered."

{ 4 }

THE TRIP TO ROSINGS PARK was not long, but it was nearly twice as long as the time it would take on horseback, and as such, James felt a trifle restless in the carriage. The time was not improved by Anne's flushed face, sniffles, shivers, and occasional cough.

"You are ill," James said finally. "We really ought to have stayed at home where you would not be exposed to the cold and damp. I do believe that hot water bottle is doing nothing for you."

"I do not feel well, it is true, but we shall be there presently." Her voice was hoarse. "I would not miss the christening; what an insult to Charlotte."

"You must not think your friends so ready to take insult. I believe people are largely more charitable in nature than you expect."

Anne was silent. James realized belatedly that Lady Catherine was perhaps not a good example of universal charity. Or of someone who overlooked slights.

Anne shivered again and James moved to sit beside her on the forward-facing bench of the carriage. He put his arm around her thin shoulders and held her left hand in his right. Even through her pelisse, she felt cold against his side. Her fingers, though gloved, felt frigid.

"Good gracious, you are like ice."

James didn't notice how stiff she grew in his half-embrace; from his point of view, she was always so. "We shall send you to bed as soon as we arrive at Rosings. Perhaps you will be well enough on Saturday for the christening. Old Joseph declares we shall have a warm spell and he is generally to be believed."

At Rosings, they were admitted by Lady Catherine's august butler, a man with rather more dignity than most dukes James had met, and James immediately commanded him to have Anne's maid escort her to her room.

"Lady Catherine desires—" the man began.

"Yes, but she don't know Anne is ill. Do as I say, that's a good man."

James, for all his good-heartedness, was a gentleman born and had an air that immediately overbore the most pretentious of servants.

Anne was tenderly escorted up to her room, and James was announced alone in Lady Catherine's fine drawing room. The sun slanted in the many small panes that made up the tall windows. Lady Catherine looked much as before, if perhaps a trifle grayer and more lined.

She was not alone, thus James was spared a prolonged tête-à-tête. The other occupants of the room were Mr. Collins, the parson, and Mr. and Mrs. Darcy. James was not an overly sensitive man, but even he felt that a certain awkwardness pervaded the room.

Mr. Collins rose with alacrity and bowed deeply to James. "Welcome Mr. Sutherland. I hope you know that I am deeply honored by your presence for the christening that shall shortly bless my humble family. My wife and I are very conscious of the condescension and cannot enough express our appreciation. That Miss de Bourgh—Mrs. Sutherland, I mean!—such a superior and well-born young lady, should stoop to be godmother to my own daughter quite overpowers me. Indeed—"

"Yes, yes, of course," James said, unable to listen to the man go on much longer. "She's quite happy to do so, Collins. Very fond of your wife, happy to oblige."

"But where is my daughter?" Lady Catherine demanded.

James explained and she sighed knowingly.

"If I had had the management of her, I should have most straightly warned her not to overtire herself. Truly, she ought to have prepared for the christening and taken extra pains not to become ill just now, but then it is not her doing, her constitution was ever so. Almost perverse in its inconvenience. Only the most diligent care and notice on my part prevented her from being constantly ill. I daresay the same child in another family would not have survived past infancy."

"How do you do, sir?" Mr. Darcy said, when there did not seem to be much more said on that topic.

"Excellent, thank you. I've not had the pleasure since your wedding." He bowed to the lady. "Mrs. Darcy. You're looking well. Marriage agrees with you."

Mrs. Darcy twinkled. "Thank you, sir, it does. And do call me Elizabeth, or even Lizzy, if you please; we are family now."

Lady Catherine gave an outraged and all-too-audible, "Humph."

James took a seat.

There was silence until Mr. Collins cleared his throat. "Mr. Sutherland, you must allow me to tell you that Hunsford is diminished through your good fortune. My humble congregation still feels the lack of the delicate beauty your wife so long graced us with."

James eyed the man. He was a parson, was he not? What was all this about Anne's beauty?

Lady Catherine sniffed. "Mr. Sutherland, my daughter tells me you are quite the agriculturalist. An experimental home farm, I believe."

"Yes, indeed. The gains made in English agriculture the last fifty years have been meteoric, but I believe there is still progress to be made, still advances yet to be found."

"Advancements are all very good, if they are indeed *advancements*, which I fear too often they are not. If you would be advised by me," her voice left no uncertainty about his wishes, "you would be content to follow the traditions of your father and grandfather. Or even Mr. Darcy, if only a contemporary subject will do for you. Mr. Darcy does not weary himself or his land with the strange methods and unnecessary expenditure of these unconventional practices."

Mr. Darcy cleared his throat. "I do not, it is true, but I am not sure I ought to be praised for it. The truth is that having many properties to oversee, both those I inherited and those of which I am a trustee," he nodded to Lady Catherine, "I simply have not the time or attention to give to such a project."

"And too much sense to try it," Lady Catherine said decisively.

James shrugged affably. "As you say. I enjoy it prodigiously, and it may as well be those who find joy in it who undertake the task. It certainly was a steep expenditure, but I have high hopes. And if I should make any measurable, reproduceable progress, I should publish it in the county reports, so that Mr. Darcy, and any other farmer, could make what use of it they will."

"I have no opinion of the county reports or this new Board of Agriculture," Lady Catherine stated. "They slavishly worship Coke, you know, and he is nothing more than an overrated, pompous commoner. He is a Whig to boot, devoted to Fox, and we all know what a fanatical loon he was. The man supported the American patriots; he dressed in Washington's colors! My husband said hanging was too good for him."

"That's as may be, Lady Catherine," James said, "but Coke did not do any of those things. And whether it is Coke or his bailiff, someone up there has done remarkable things with selective breeding. I am currently seeing whether I cannot crossbreed his Leicester sheep with our long-legged Kentish ewes."

"What will that accomplish?" Lizzy asked.

"Well, you see, ours take a good eighteen months longer to mature, and with animal husbandry, that is a while. The Norfolk variety were similar, but Coke has been selectively breeding to create a tame, superior breed that grows well off turnips and matures younger. I fancy our Kentish wool is the finer, however. If I am successful, perhaps I may marry the best of both qualities."

Lady Catherine did not ever admit interest or approval of the conversation, but she did not stop it, so

James spent some minutes happily explaining the chief interest of his life. He could talk at length on the four-crop rotation, the benefits of the Scottish turnip, the milking capacity of various cows, and more, but he stopped himself before too long. Darcy appeared interested, but it could not possibly be of much interest to Lizzy, Lady Catherine, or the parson.

"There, I must stop myself or I will put you all to sleep," James said. "Poor Anne must put up with me now, but I know better than to go boring on for more than a quarter of an hour, which it nearly has been."

"No, you manage to make it quite interesting, sir," Lizzy said. "Darcy continually tells me I may make what changes I will at Pemberley," an indeterminate noise from Lady Catherine was politely ignored, "and perhaps this is the thing. I think I should enjoy breeding sheep."

"You shall have a flock of the new Leicesters, if you still desire it in the spring," Darcy said.

"You mean, if I remember in spring. You make capital out of my impulsive nature."

Darcy smiled, rather teasingly. "Do I not deserve the credit for generosity, regardless?"

A dimple appeared in Lizzy's cheek. "I suppose you do. But I warn you I am tenacious of memory."

"Do I not know it?"

James rather thought he would have kissed her had they not an audience. No wonder Lady Catherine had accused Lizzy of enticing the man—the pair still smelled of April and May!

"But we should be going," Lizzy said. "I daresay Charlotte will be looking out for us soon."

Mr. Collins was all protest. "My dear Charlotte would never wish to *rush* Mr. Darcy or to rob Lady Catherine of the company of her nephew, I assure you. Think nothing of her needs."

Lizzy looked a little vexed. Mr. Darcy took her hand and stood. "No, we ought to return to the parsonage in good time. Good afternoon, Mr. Sutherland."

James was no idiot, but it took him a moment to understand that Mr. and Mrs. Darcy were staying at the parsonage, *not* at Rosings Park. He stifled a sigh. So much for Anne's overtures to her mother.

Lady Catherine appeared to do battle with herself. Her grayish cheeks turned a mottled red. "You will all come back for dinner," she said finally. "And Charlotte, if she is finally feeling well enough. I will send the carriage."

Mr. Collins wrung his hands. "How considerate, Lady Catherine. What an honor, when I have been sitting half the day with you already. My dear Charlotte shall be happy to come, I am sure; she recovers apace."

James chanced a look at Lizzy, and he was willing to wager a monkey that Charlotte would not be dragged

out to a prolonged dinner on a cold evening if Lizzy had
anything to say about it.

{ 5 }

THE EVENING WAS COMPRISED of the same party, as neither Anne nor Charlotte made an appearance. James made sure that Anne was resting, and Lizzy had apparently done the same by Charlotte. By the parson's conduct, however, you would hardly know his wife was missing, while he mentioned Anne in nearly every breath.

In the morning, when James looked in on Anne, he found her bundled up before the fire in her room.

"I must tell you," he said jovially, "that if Mr. Collins was not a parson, I should suspect him of having designs upon you. If he mentions your delicate beauty again, I may need to call him out. I warn you I shall be alert for any *flirting* on his part."

She barely smiled at his teasing; the dreadful blankness was back in her face.

"Should you be out of bed?" James asked. "Ought you to be resting?"

"I am not feverish this morning," Anne said. "I think I shall be well enough for the christening tomorrow."

Her chair was made of shiny cherry wood with cheerful pink chintz cushions, but she sat in it limply. Her head was tilted back and to the side, as if her neck could not be troubled to hold it up.

"Do you feel very unwell?" James asked. There was a high-backed wooden chair across from her, and he sat in it gingerly. It was what he thought of as a prim old woman's chair.

"No, not bad. Just... weak." Anne sighed. To his dismay, tears gathered in her eyes.

"Don't cry," James said. "We'll get you to the church if I have to carry you in."

"I hope that won't be necessary but thank you." Tears still slipped down her cheeks.

James pulled his handkerchief from the inner pocket of his vest. Sometimes when he was out at the farm and the hay was up and the ozone heavy, he would sneeze like a man in a convulsion, so he always kept one with him.

"I am sorry." She gently blotted her face with it. "I am feeling rather low and distressed for no good reason. I have been so well since the summer, that I am quite cast down to return to normal. I should not have expected it to last forever."

"Well, no, not likely. But then... everyone said you picked up wonderful after Tunbridge. Perhaps we should take you again. Or I could have a wagon sent to bring back several barrels of the water to Middlefinch. Do you think we could make tea with it?"

Anne chuckled weakly. "Would that we could! I detested drinking that tepid, rusty water; tea would have been an immense improvement."

"But if the water facilitated your health..."

"I suppose it might have. But the water is said to lose its properties if you store it or boil it. Perhaps I could drink it merely warmed, if we did visit," Anne mused. "I did learn that some young ladies demanded the water heated. It was put in a bottle with an airtight cork and placed in hot water."

"Was anything else done for you in Tunbridge? Warm baths? Tonics?"

"None of that. The doctor did give me some powders when I had an asthmatic fit. I drank the first dose, but he made up the rest of the mixture into pills, which I took for some days."

"We must have more," James exclaimed. "Perhaps therein was the key to your improved constitution."

"But I finished them weeks ago and I have not had such a fit lately," Anne said.

"No, but perhaps that is a lingering effect. What was in the powder?"

"I do not recollect perfectly; I was very ill that night. My mother, or Elizabeth, might know. I believe iron was some part of it, perhaps an aromatic powder as well."

"Iron. Well, of course," James said, slapping his knee. "Why did I not think of that? When a set of piglets are pale and wheezy, everyone knows you best up the iron in the sow. Some even swab the teats with iron paste so the pigs will take it in. I have been wondering myself whether a little iron solution, trickled into their mouths, wouldn't work faster."

Anne's brow furrowed. "Piglets?"

"We must have that doctor to consult. Excuse me, my dear. I must speak with your aunt."

Lady Catherine was less amenable than James expected.

"I conversed with Dr. Blackburn for a month before our trip, through the post, and yet his diagnosis was the green-sickness." She scoffed. "Of all the foolishness. He gave his opinion very decidedly, although everyone knows green-sickness is a symptom of chlorotic girls who live in crowded cities and sit in hot rooms till late hours of the night and eat poorly. Anne has never had such an unhealthy lifestyle or diet, nor is she melancholic."

James had his own opinion on Anne's melancholy, but he kept that to himself. "I don't pretend to know the illnesses particular to young ladies, but I cannot help but think his prescription may have done some good. Would it not be worth a trial? A second test, to see if his antidote is again beneficial?"

"The *waters* of Tunbridge were the beneficial factor for Anne; I knew it would be so. I have no opinion of Dr. Blackburn. What is more," she looked triumphant, "green-sickness starts when a girl becomes a lady, and Anne has been ill since infancy."

"Her condition does not seem a match, then," James agreed.

"Exactly."

"But even a broken clock is right twice a day. I may consult with this Dr. Blackburn. Do you have any other objections to the man?"

James's voice was at all times respectful, but Lady Catherine could not like the tone of his conversation this morning. There was a something in his voice that invited her to say what she would but offered no compliance. It was not condescension, but it verged on playful indulgence. Lady Catherine would not be *indulged.* James would get no better advice anywhere than from her, particularly on the subject of her own daughter's constitution! Of course, Lady Catherine prided herself on being a decisive, efficient, and resourceful woman on any number of troubles, but surely her expertise on Anne was unassailable.

"No objections, I'm sure," Lady Catherine said, at her most icy.

Unaware of the deeper disapprobation he had incurred, James took his leave. After assuring himself that Anne was as well as could be, he took his pocketbook, went to the stables, and saddled his horse.

The sun was a pale white in a cream November sky. The sunlight was soft but effective, warming his back under his dark blue riding coat. Beautiful day for a good long ride and Tunbridge Wells was well within riding distance of Rosings Park. No time like the present, what?

Anne was conscious of a slight loneliness when James left her room, but the impression was mild, and quickly dropped away as she watched the block of sunshine on the colorful carpet slowly creep across the floor. As it inched in a shallow arc, lighting up the woven flowers, Anne managed to stop thinking of anything.

It was some hours later that Anne, after dozing fitfully in her chair, halfheartedly sipping several half-cups of tea, and answering her mother's proxy inquiries through her maid, finally left her room for the drawing room.

"Ah, you join me at last," Lady Catherine said. "I do not complain, but it has been strangely quiet, I declare. Not a soul from the parsonage has sent word today or come nigh the house. And James went for a ride quite early and has not been seen since."

"I hope you have not been lonely," Anne said.

"Lonely? I should think not. I have enough to do; I don't fancy myself into such moods."

"Have you seen Charlotte? How does she fare?" Anne asked. "She wrote cheerfully, but so she always does."

"I have not seen her since the child was born. But according to Collins there is nothing amiss with her except an overabundance of caution. Charlotte Collins is a hard-working young woman, I must say, which makes it all the more surprising that she should coddle herself and the babe so. When I see her, I shall tell her straightly that it will not do. Infants must be hardened to cold to make them vigorous and strong."

"She did write that the doctor advised her to avoid drafts and rich food—which might both be experienced in visiting us here at Rosings."

Anne did not realize that she had contradicted her mother—she was merely explaining the doctor's words, sharing the circumstances—but Lady Catherine, still rankling from her conversation with James, swelled a little.

"I hope I know as much as that nincompoop Doctor Farnley. All the modern doctors and *accoucheurs* are the same; they would have every lady lying in for months *before* birth and stifled to her eyes for months *after.* I myself am a proponent of the cold bath for infants; certainly, the harm of a hot bath is self-evident, and it stands to God-given reason that the opposite would be valuable. If you had been strong enough for such a course, I daresay it would have considerably relieved your symptoms."

"Yes, Mother," Anne agreed, "perhaps it would."

"Now, tell me," Lady Catherine ordered, "how you have been faring at Middlefinch?"

"James is teaching me to play chess—"

"No, no. I mean, how is your health?"

Anne felt oddly deflated. "It is as normal..."

It was nearly time to dress for dinner when James returned. He bowed to Lady Catherine and greeted Anne with a kiss on the cheek and a hearty smile. "Good news, my dear." He withdrew a flat glass bottle from his coat pocket, swirling the water inside. "I have several of these for the next few days, and three barrels are on their way to Middlefinch."

"Did you—did you go to Tunbridge Wells *today*?" Anne asked, quite thrown.

"Yes! Not far you know, on horseback. A few hours there and back again and the whole matter is settled. I wonder that more people don't order it for themselves. They gave me quite the rigamarole about the necessity of pulling it fresh from the spring, but that sounds rather too convenient to me. Want to keep a lid on it, they do, keep us nobs coming to them!" He laughed happily. "But if you ask me, what's in the water is *in* it, it can't get out once you bottle it up safely. So, I had my way in the end, which I usually do."

"I—thank you," Anne said. "I didn't realize you meant to execute the project immediately." She was rather dreading the water—it often left her nauseated— but she also felt an unaccustomed lightness.

"No time like the present, and here at Rosings we're nearly halfway there already."

"Did you see Dr. Blackburn as well?" Lady Catherine asked coldly.

"Yes, I did, and he is what you said, ma'am; extremely puffed up in his own opinions! But for all that, I think he may have stumbled on something helpful, so I had him make up a month's worth of his powders for Anne." He held up a hand. "You don't like it that I did so, and I don't blame you—the man is not conciliating—but we must be scientific about this. I am not a professional man of science, but what those fellows are doing now... even a country gentleman like myself can understand it.

If you want to understand the utility of something, you must methodically test it in different circumstance, putting aside personal bias and observing without prejudice."

Lady Catherine, for whom the mere idea of putting aside personal bias was an offence, was nearly stricken dumb. "You will... *experiment*... on my daughter? I think not, sir."

"Not in the sense you are picturing," he assured her kindly.

"In *no* sense. Make no mistake—"

During an angry intake of breath, James cut in, a hint of steel in his voice. "I didn't intend to anger you, but I, as her husband, must be the best judge of what she may or may not try. Second only to herself, of course, I would never force anything upon Anne."

Anne laid a cold hand on his knee; James did not know whether she meant it as warning, thanks, or merely distraction.

He placed his over her own, again smiling warmly at Lady Catherine. "Come, let us not brangle. My mother says I am mad after science. When you and she next meet you may excoriate me to the skies, and I will not lift a finger in my defense."

Even Lady Catherine was not immune to his sincere frankness. She sniffed. "Science! Perhaps you ought to have been a chemist or an astronomer, sir."

If it was meant to be cutting, James did not take it that way. "In another life, I would leap at the chance. Do you at all follow the work of Sir Humphry Davy? He has taken the town by storm these last years. I myself enjoyed several of his lectures in '09. 'Nothing is so dangerous to the progress of the human mind,' he said, 'than to assume that our views of science are ultimate, that there are no mysteries in nature, that our triumphs are complete, and that there are no new worlds to conquer.'"

The grand words opened another window in Anne's mind. That night as she lay in bed, her feet cold despite the warming pan that had been swiped through the sheets, the poetry of unknown worlds, mysteries, and triumphs guided her to sleep.

{ 6 }

J AMES FOUND THE CHRISTENING what every christening was: much fancy fuss over a squirming, unhappy infant. James was quite fond of his own son,
Barney, but couldn't pretend to any great feeling for
other children of his limited acquaintance. Infants, in
particular, were opaque to him. Not only did their crying render them off-putting, but he could not suppose
that his approbation, if gained, would mean anything to
them. He and the infant were entirely indifferent to one
another's opinion or goodwill.

Mr. Collins conducted the ceremony while Mrs. Collins sat in the front row, just in front of him. Mr. and
Mrs. Darcy, along with Anne, stood in the front as the
baby girl—named Catherine, as one might expect, after
Lady Catherine—was prayed over and blessed and so on.
James had thought it odd that the mother was not more
involved in the ceremony, but so it had been at Barney's

christening as well; the whole ceremony was fronted by the godparents.

The lesson was overly long, but other than that, Collins could not muck it up much. Before James was more than moderately stiff, and wondering whether Anne ought to sit, Collins was turning to the congregation. "People of God, will you welcome this child and uphold her in her new life in Christ?"

"With the help of God, we will," they answered. The ceremony ended with a final prayer.

James was not afflicted by any great sentimentality at the sight of Anne holding the babe. He would not mind having more children, but with Anne being unwell, it was not likely that she would bear a pregnancy well, or the rigor of childbirth. They had consummated their marriage like Christians, of course, but James had been more than a little relieved that she had not gotten with child and had not gone to her much since.

Anne passed the baby to Mrs. Darcy and made her way to Charlotte. James was reminded of Anne's comment that she knew Charlotte, not the baby, and smiled.

Soon the family party removed to the parsonage, excepting only Lady Catherine, who went inexorably home despite much urging to the contrary, and much to Mr. Collins's dismay. After seeing the lay of the land, James was surprised that the man had been coerced into hous-

ing Lizzy and Darcy at all, so morbidly did he dread Lady Catherine's displeasure.

A neat and tidy luncheon of cold meat, tongue pie, and such filling but humble food was soon served. It was not lavish, but adequate and done with propriety, of which James gave Charlotte the credit.

Several of Charlotte's family were also present, her mother and father and three of her numerous siblings. Of these latter, James wrinkled his nose. He had not forgotten his plan to install one of Charlotte's sisters as a companion or aide-de-camp to Anne, but these fe-males—for girls they hardly were—would not do.

Maria was a sweet simpleton. She could not forbear cooing over the baby's long christening gown, which was tolerable, and assuring Anne that Lady Catherine's method of packing was ever so superior, and that Maria would never forget the lesson Lady Catherine had once given her on the folding of a muslin, which was not tol-erable.

The next sister, Hester, was crying copiously. James was not sure why, but it was not propitious.

The third sister, Molly, at first seemed a viable op-tion. She answered his how-do-you-do sensibly enough. He expressed joy that Charlotte and her daughter had done so well for the first weeks of the child's life.

Molly nodded seriously and lowered her voice. "Yes. Do you know, I sent *dear* Charlotte my own charm for warding off evil, and I am sure it has done it! I must make another for the *dear* baby straight away. Do you know that whooping cough can be cured by passing a child thrice under and over the belly of a donkey, boiling three of its hairs in three tablespoons of milk, and feeding it to the child for three consecutive mornings?"

James knew nothing of the sort, and his methodical soul recoiled at crude superstition. He would not install such a girl in his household if he could help it. Obie was already enough to try a saint, but at least he generally knew his effusions were a fiction.

Perhaps this was why Anne had not greeted his idea about Charlotte's sisters with eagerness, and he could hardly blame her.

Ah, well. He would find another way.

Anne mostly sat near the fire after the luncheon. Mr. Darcy likewise was seated nearby, but he scarce took his nose out of a journal so was hardly an ideal companion. James joined Anne presently, and Lizzy drifted over as well.

"And how do you find life at Middlefinch?" Lizzy asked Anne. "Did you adjust at once? I am still in shock every morning that I wake at Pemberley, but perhaps for you it is not so very different."

They made desultory conversation about their homes and the weather—for once Kent and Middlefinch were colder than Derbyshire and Pemberley!—and then Anne mentioned Obie. "James's uncle also resides at Middlefinch. He is a writer."

"Oh, how jealous I am!" Lizzy exclaimed. "How interesting. What does he write? Do please say gothic novels and not something truly ridiculous, like a single man's philosophical treatise on the nature of femininity."

Anne frowned in confusion over this. "I believe he writes short scary stories, ghosts and such."

"Is his name Obadiah Sutherland? Perhaps I have read something of his."

James smiled. "He uses a penname, but what it is he does not say. I know my mother paid for his first printing, but I believe he has sold several stories since—he is always sending and receiving heavy packets in the mail—but he does not speak much of it."

"A mysterious man of letters! Better and better!"

"Ought I to be jealous?" Darcy inquired dryly, looking up from his journal to smile at Lizzy.

Anne pictured the narrow-shouldered, stoop-backed Obie and laughed aloud. She clapped a hand over her mouth.

James chuckled as well. "Don't be sorry, Anne, the image amuses. If you could meet my uncle, Lizzy— indeed, I hope you both will visit us next year and do so!—you will see that he is more mouse than mystery."

Anne had never seen Charlotte cry, but when she opened the package of silver cups from Anne during a quiet moment, a few tears welled up.

She truly was delighted. "Why, these are so fine. Just beautiful. Very like the ones my mother prizes from her grandmother."

"Yes, I saw hers when we visited your family in Hertfordshire."

"How observant you are!" It had taken Charlotte many months to stop thinking of Anne as "Miss de Bourgh" and even longer to realize that Anne truly valued Charlotte's friendship. Anne was not easy to get to know, but moments like this reminded Charlotte that there was more to her than met the eye.

Charlotte could not pretend to have the deep friendship with Anne that she had with Lizzy, but she was cognizant that Anne had no closer friend than herself. This was both a compliment and a weight, as there was very little Charlotte could do to show her friendship to Anne. But Charlotte was both sensible and kind, and she knew she could at least reciprocate with heartfelt thanks.

"So thoughtful." Charlotte squeezed Anne's hands. "What a kind gift. You are a good friend." Over Anne's shoulder, James gave Charlotte a grateful nod and smile.

"You are very welcome. I am relieved that you are well," Anne said. She blinked and wiped a few of her own tears away. "I prayed for you every night in October."

"How faithful," Charlotte said. "Even Lizzy probably only prayed for me once or twice, if she remembered at all."

Lizzy, who had approached to see the gift, laughed. "Guilty. But I mentioned you to Georgiana and I am sure she prayed enough for both of us. Between her and Miss de Bourgh—I'm sorry, Mrs. Sutherland—your heavenly petitions were covered."

"How is Georgiana?" Charlotte asked.

"She is well." Lizzy twinkled as if she had a secret. "In fact, she is soon to be engaged."

"She is?" Anne asked, startled. "Prior to her season?"

"Yes, but I ought not say more at present; it will be official at Christmas."

Mr. Collins now joined the group. "A set of teapots! Very—"

"Caudle cups," Charlotte corrected quickly.

"Of course. A set of caudle cups! Very fine and such an honor. Mrs. Collins and I will be able to say, 'These caudle cups were a gift from our dear friend, Mrs. Sutherland, the daughter of Lady Catherine!' I am sure I never expected life to hold such a delightful surprise as a set of caudle cups from the daughter of my esteemed patron. And Mr. Sutherland, as well," he bowed to that gentleman. "You have been such a friend to us. Thank you for these delightful caudle cups, sir."

Charlotte rather thought if he said the words *caudle cups* again, she might shriek. But her capacity for nonsense had been increased.

She merely smiled. "Thank you, Mr. Sutherland."

James took his place beside Anne, holding his wife's hand and smoothing his thumb over it. "Not at all. Nothing to say about it. All Anne's doing."

"That I can well believe," Mr. Collins said. "Mrs. Sutherland has always had such delicate sensibilities, which, dare I say, match her delicate beauty."

James turned a wry look upon the parson. "Take care, Collins, you're dashed close to dallying with my wife under my very nose."

Mr. Collins could not have been more surprised if James had accused him of adultery. "I—I—"

A gleam of humor shone in James's eyes. "Save the plaudits for your own bride. Don't know when I've seen a such a rosy-cheeked, good-looking new mother."

Mr. Collins furrowed his brow.

"See? That's some of your own for you." James chuckled.

Charlotte could not forbear thinking that Anne was extremely fortunate in her choice of husband. Humor, sense, and goodwill seemed united in him. But Charlotte was not wistful. Humor, sense, and goodwill were no less united in herself; therefore, Charlotte was merely happy for Anne rather than bitterly envious.

James would also have made an unexceptional husband for Georgiana, now Charlotte thought of it, but apparently Georgiana had another attachment, so it was just as well that Anne got him. Charlotte was a little surprised that Georgiana should have entered an engagement so quickly, and someone she had not mentioned in her letters, unless... good gracious, could it be the painter? The Darcy family would be fraught with interest if that were so. They were still weathering the disgrace of Lydia's aborted elopement and sudden marriage.

Charlotte shook her head and looked about her at her own tidy house, her stout daughter, and her happy party. She had many blessings.

She retreated from the front room presently to care for the baby. She and Mr. Collins were not so positioned as to afford a wet-nurse, and she did not mind. The time alone with Baby Catherine was special and Charlotte thought, when sufficient months had passed to make the delivery fade somewhat, she would quite like to have more children.

Mr. Collins was what he was, neither wise nor evil, but the children would be hers to love and train. And little Catherine, as a daughter, with Lizzy and Anne as her godmothers, had as good a chance as any girl of her station to achieve a good position.

With a startled laugh, Charlotte realized she would soon turn into Mrs. Bennet if she did not take care.

ANNE FOUND HER RETURN to Middlefinch surprisingly pleasant.—Barney was boisterously
happy to see his father. When they drove up to
the house, it seemed to Anne that he would run nearly
under the wheels of the carriage. He stopped precipi-
tously on the flagstones short of the carriageway. His
father snatched him up and tossed him into the air, de-
manding what he had been about, to Barney's shrill cries
of delight. James did not forget his wife for long, however, and quickly turned to help her out of the carriage
and into the house without delay.

Barney eyed her progress dubiously. "Are you ill now
that it's winter? Will you be so until spring?"

James shushed him. "No, of course she will not. We
must not tire her."

"He is not impertinent," Anne explained. "I told him
that was often the way of things."

She did indeed remain sickly for a time, and kept to her room some four days upon returning from Rosings to Middlefinch. But instead of the fever and congestion settling into her head and chest, it seemed to pass. She drank warm water from Tunbridge with her breakfasts and a dose of Dr. Blackburn's powders made up into pills with luncheon and supper. James anticipated the results with more optimism than Anne did, but some of his optimism was perhaps communicated to her, for she began to feel that, even should the powders prove useless and the water ineffective, James would try something else, until he hit upon something that alleviated her symptoms.

Barney, of course, did not invade her room while she was sick, but when she quitted it, he found a way down to the drawing room with rather more regularity than he probably ought. The third time he showed up, his brown head appearing half in the doorway, with one bright amber eye darting to her before quickly drawing back, Anne pursed her lips. "Good day, Barney."

"Hullo."

"Is it Nurse's day off, or is it that she has fallen asleep again?"

He came around the corner. "It is that Mrs. Gridley told Nurse 'on no account to consider that she was blamed for her nephew's unchristian treatment of...' of somebody named Rachel," Barney quoted carefully. "But that made Nurse spitting mad. They is argufying now."

"They are *arguing*, you mean?"

Barney agreed with this. "They are arguing good."

"They are arguing *well*," Anne corrected, but then realized this was probably not the best conversation for a grammar lesson. "Never mind."

Barney took Anne's hand as they again climbed the stairs to the nursery. "I am to have plum cake for tea," Barney said. "You may have a piece if it will not ruin your dinner."

Anne smiled. "That is kind of you."

"Will you stop 'em fightin'?" Barney asked.

"Yes."

If Anne thought it would require any ingenuity or forceful reprimand to end the argument, she was incorrect. The ladies were already parting, Mrs. Gridley rather red and Nurse rather yellow.

"Now, see," Nurse snapped at the housekeeper as she swept away. "You have made me forsake my duties and Barney has gone and disturbed the mistress again. *Unchristian treatment,* indeed."

Mrs. Gridley stopped short and sketched a quick curtsey to Anne. "Good day, ma'am. If it is convenient, I will come take my orders at the usual time."

Anne inclined her head.

"As for you, Master Barney," Nurse turned to him, "if you would not immediately slip away as soon as my eye was off you, that would a be a heavenly blessing!"

"Heavenly blessing or not," Anne said firmly, "I must insist that your duties do *not* include allowing your charge to slip away four or five days out of seven."

"No, ma'am, no, and I do apologize that he has been plaguing you. Master James was the same, but he would always sneak down to the stables or kennels. I do not know why Barney will keep bothering you."

Put in that way, Anne felt a slight glow. She was... flattered? Touched? Anne was apparently chosen *over* other amusement; she had not considered that aspect of Barney's truant visits.

"Perhaps if I was to come daily to the nursery, as my health permits, Barney would not feel the need to come to me."

"Yes, ma'am. That would be a treat for him, though whether it will solve my problem I do not know. Mayhap he will find some other place to sneak away to."

Anne looked at Barney. "Will you stop sneaking away from Nurse if I promise to come visit you in the mornings?"

He replied with great dignity, "I do not sneak away; this is my own house." His façade cracked a little. "Besides which, I don't even always mean it. Only I think of a place I would rather be and before I know it, I am halfway there."

Nurse sighed. "That is true and true. When I'm a-watching him, I stop him nigh on fifty times a day from wandering off."

"Perhaps that's as far as we shall get today," Anne said, stumbling upon the wisdom of not building Rome in a day.

"But will you eat the plum-cake?" Barney tugged on her hand.

"I do not overly care for plum-cake, but I will join you for tea." Anne followed him to his small table.

"You don't like it?" Barney held her chair properly as she sat. His voice was awed. "You must be a most picksome eater then, for Nurse says as I am most aggravating, and at least I will *always* eat plum-cake."

"Silly boy. I am not a picksome eater. I merely do not have a large appetite. Also, overly sweet things I generally find repulsive, and overly spiced things are not good for my stomach." She eyed his sturdy frame. "You do not look as if you are suffering from your pickiness. I daresay that is attributable to overindulgence in plum-cake."

"Perhaps if you try it again, you will like it," Barney offered. "Perhaps it will help you not be so skinny."

"For shame!" Nurse cried. "Watch your tongue, Master Barney."

Barney begged pardon. "I did not intend to be *rag-mannered.*"

"I trust not," Anne said severely. "In the meantime, perhaps we had better have an occupation for your mind and tongue. What lessons have you begun, sir? Or do you still fritter away your time as an infant?"

Barney looked justifiably injured. "'Course I have lessons. I have my primer, and Nurse teaches me in... in Lit'rature, Mathematics, and... and languages."

Nurse looked slightly startled at this description, and Barney expanded. "Literature is just books, and we read lots of books; and mathematics is only arithmetic, and of course she teaches me numbers on my slate."

"And languages?"

He quoted a German passage that sounded rather fierce.

"Goodness. And the translation?" Anne inquired.

"The dead men lie bathed in the weltering blood, And the living are blent in the slippery flood," he said with gusto.

Anne looked to Nurse.

"My grandma was German," she said, a little defiantly. "I wasn't educated to learn much French, but I know some German and I have a book of poetry I read from."

Anne nodded. "A knowledge of German is certainly worth instilling."

"What did you study when you were a child?" Barney asked.

"French and English, which I learned from my governess. A little arithmetic... I was too ill for much tutoring." Anne flushed. This was something her mother frequently said when explaining Anne's lack of accomplishments in the usual feminine attainments. Anne had never thought of it overly, but suddenly, before a somewhat sweaty, grubby little boy, she felt embarrassed.

She pushed the thought away, and though she declined the plum cake, she did take a biscuit, which made Barney smile around his own rich treat.

{ 8 }

**B**ARNEY WAS NOT THE ONLY ONE who sought her out. Though his visits were unpredictable, Obie seemed to find his way down to the drawing room more often than he had before.

"Might I join you?" he would ask, gentleman-like in manner if sometimes confused in mind. If Anne wished to stay alone, she could remain in her room, part of which was fitted as a sitting room, so it did not seem appropriate to forbid him the drawing room.

And he was generally quiet, pulling out his messy manuscript in the light of the window and then staring at it absently for a good half hour, sometimes sucking on the end of his quill with a soft squelching noise.

Soft mutters would morph into sentences as he began to write. He seemed to be the sort who had to vocalize to form thoughts into coherency. Snatches of strange description and melodramatic dialogue would reach her.

"...his mother wept, 'Do you deny that the very color of Hades has entered thy face, painting it in infernal reds and blacks, such that thy visage rivals Mephistopheles? Your soul is forfeit if she feeds on you for even one more night. You are nearly lost to me already..." Obie's dry voice was a most strange vehicle for such lofty words.

And soon thereafter, "...her scream rose as a scale played by the clumsy fingers of a schoolgirl, halting and jagged, and yet ending on a note that all understood as being the end. As indeed it was the end, could she but know it."

Anne could not ignore his utterances, for they painted pictures that insisted on forming themselves before her mind's eye, interposing strange scenes before the fire she observed, the chess game she practiced, or the letter she composed.

She could not forbear correcting Obie when he called her Mary, for it made her feel uncomfortable, but she tried otherwise to be conciliating. Indeed, she occasionally found herself disappointed when he joined her, and his muttering showed that she had missed a climactic event.

Lady Beatrice was always matter of fact; but she and Anne did not have much to say to one another, and so had little conversation beyond the weather and various household matters. Anne did not even know that Lady

Beatrice contemplated the purchase of a new horse until James broached the topic at the supper table.

"Old Joseph told me Timothy is up near Edinburgh bringing back a new stud."

Lady Beatrice wiped her mouth. "Yes. Lord Nutley put me in the way of it. I saw Golden Breeze race at Edgeham, do you recall? First by five seconds; nothing like it. But he is pushing seven."

"Why would Grantham sell? The foals of Golden Breeze would be worth nearly as much."

"But Grantham is all to pieces, have you not heard?"

"I imagine the competition on the sale was fierce."

Lady Beatrice looked not the slightest bit self-conscious. "But of course, my dear! Nine hundred! But it is such a coup. If I can get a foal of him by Morning Song—"

"Nine hundred?" James demanded, interrupting his mother. He so rarely spoke sharply, that Anne quite dropped her spoon in the soup.

His mother looked at him. "Well, yes, dear, at auction, you know. That is why I went up to London while you were in Hunsford. I know you said we must not incur great expense, which is why I instructed Lord Nutley not to bid on any other of Grantham's breakdowns. It is better economy to go for the best or nothing, and he quite agreed."

"That was very obliging of Lord Nutley," James said wryly. He sighed. "We must speak tomorrow."

Whether they did speak on the morrow, Anne was not in a position to know. It did seem an exorbitant amount to spend on a horse, but, while Anne did not know the particulars of James's financial state, it was generally known that he was quite well-off. Anne, of course, had had nothing to do with the marriage settlements; they had been arranged by her mother and Darcy.

What with one thing and another, it seemed but a short time until the day appointed to begin their trip to Pemberley for Christmas. On the morning of their departure, with a sharp wind blowing, Anne could smell salt and fish in the air. Middlefinch was farther east than Rosings, and closer to the ocean. A sea bird, large and black against the wintry blue sky, rode the wind currents like a skiff. He was far larger than the pheasants and wood pigeons that generally were found around Middlefinch.

Before her were two carriages. The first would carry their servants, including her maid Susan, James's man, and Nurse, plus most of their luggage. The second would hold the family and what baggage could be conveniently tied atop. James's horse was ridden by his groom, and the coachman would drive their carriage, while Timothy, the under groom, would drive the servants.

Anne was a bit dubious about having Barney ride in their coach for the many long hours—indeed, days!—of the trip, but James told her Barney could always be relegated to the servants' coach if he grew tiresome. They would travel north in easy stages.

The first stage was to London, where they spent the night at the Darcy town house. Anne had been surprised at this arrangement. James coughed and looked away. "I sold Sutherland House soon after Milly passed. Your cousin offered that we could stay here at our leisure. Excellent fellow, Darcy. But we shall hire a house for ourselves next season," he assured Anne.

The second night was spent in Northampton, and the third, unexpectedly, in a small village called Stanton under Bardon, when their carriage wheel struck a rut just wrong and splintered three spokes before the coachman could halt the horses.

"Dashed sorry," James said to Anne, who'd waited with Barney in the relatively warm, but fast-chilling carriage, while he ascertained the extent of the damage. "Shortest day of the year, too," he muttered, glancing up at the quickly darkening sky. "Barely mid-afternoon but we shall be in the dark soon, and the moon barely a sliver."

Anne and Barney squeezed into the coach with the servants. The broken wheel was removed and strapped on as well, while James and his man rode the two carriage horses. Timothy was left with the blunderbuss to defend the helpless coach and its luggage from any ill-intentioned persons.

"Does that mean *highwaymen?*" Barney asked, crawling over Nurse to look out the window. "Shall they tell him to *stand and deliver?*"

"No, he shall be fine. Do sit, Master Barney."

By this time Anne was quite chilled and even shivering. She was therefore thankful to reach the one small inn which Stanton under Bardon boasted, be it ever so small and ill-suited to catering to the gentry. The taproom was warm, though distressingly full of local farmers. It smelled of spirits and unwashed bodies. Anne kept her vinaigrette on a chain around her neck on such trips as this, and she snapped open the lid, raising it to her nose. Susan had soaked the sponge in a fresh mixture of vinegar, rose water, and a hint of perfume just this morning, and Anne inhaled it thankfully.

The room fell silent on the arrival of their large party, and Anne, unused to being gawked at, raised her chin perceptibly.

James's first priority was to get Anne to a comfortable room where she might relax, but a close second was to prevent Timothy spending a cold and possibly dangerous night alone on the road. An unfortunate mischance, but then, these things happened. James would be inclined to take it philosophically if only Anne's health and comfort were not at stake.

He was a trifle disconcerted that the small hostelry offered only four bedrooms, two of which were already taken. Even if the coachman and the groom, and perhaps even his man, bunked down in the stables, an indignity James was loath to force on his faithful, but highly proper servant, there was barely room for their party. In the end, the innkeeper offered to make the other two guests share a room, making three rooms for their party, with which James had to be satisfied.

The finest, such as it was, would be for him and Anne, the second for Nurse, Barney, and Susan, and the third for however many of his men could be bunked down in it.

With all the folderol, James still managed to escort Anne up to the bedchamber. The room was not overly warm, and he ordered the master of the house to build up the fire immediately. "And if your wife has any good blankets, another would be welcome."

Anne sat in the hard chair near the fire, quite trembling with cold and weariness, and James bit his lip. "I am sorry to rush off and leave you, my dear, but I really must see about replacing those spokes. I daresay half the town is in the taproom, so I have high hopes of finding a wheelwright on the instant. Once I have seen this business on the way to settled, I shall rejoin you. I will have the woman bring up tea."

After liberally motivating the village carpenter—who seemed to be wheelwright and blacksmith as well—to go back to his workshop and light his lamps for a couple hours hard labor, James returned to see how Anne fared. He was pleased to see that she had drunk some tea and lain down on the bed, hard and unappealing as it appeared. He slipped away so as not to wake her. Next, he looked in on Barney, happily eating a wrinkled winter apple their humble hostess had supplied. Finally he went to the stables to check that the horses were being well-cared for. After all this, James finally allowed himself to sit in the taproom, stretch out his legs, and call for a tankard of homebrewed.

Tiring business, traveling. With any luck, they would reach Pemberley by midafternoon on the morrow. Perhaps he should not have allowed Anne to accept this invitation from Lizzy, but she had been rather set on it. James hadn't questioned her further, but he suspected that her motivation had something to do with holding her head high before the family and friends who knew Darcy had chosen Lizzy over herself. She might say that the circumstances did not bother her, but it would be a very odd female who could resist showing that she had managed her life very well despite such a disappointment.

In addition, Anne's health had seemed moderately better in the last weeks. James very much hoped it was due to the new regimen he had procured for her, but he was aware of the perilous ease of misidentifying coincidence as proof—the very definition of superstition—and he was therefore withholding judgement.

His repose did not last long. In fact, it was merely a drop in what transpired to be a long evening, particularly as James felt it right to return to the carriage with the coachman when the wheel was finally complete.

There was nothing like a late-night ride on an unfamiliar stretch of road, with the forest close in on the right and fog-covered fields to the left, to make England feel quite mysterious. Indeed, they were not far from Nottingham, the site of James's favorite folk tales of Robin Hood and his merry men.

Obie would have some fantastical way of describing it, James was sure, but being a prosaic man himself, James merely the slapped the reins and urged the horse on.

When eventually James returned to the inn, he was glad to find that Anne had risen to eat a late dinner. He was also glad to partake of a somewhat heavier dinner himself.

"You must be famished," Anne said. She had resumed her place by the fire and finally removed her cloak and pelisse, which James took to mean she was warm at last.

"Yes, but all's well that ends well," he said comfortably, working his way through the food provided. "Timothy is a good lad. He was sitting there whistling and stamping his feet when we arrived, game to the bottom. It was some to-do to get that wheel back on. The carriage was listing, and it took all three of us to hoist the corner high enough that we might shove the wheel into place. Glad I went with them."

"Yes. And I suppose it is too late to travel onward now."

James speared his fork into a fresh bannock, a round Scottish bread, and spread it with butter. "At this hour? Yes, much too late. But we'll be on our way in the morning. I know this inn is not much—is that a cornhusk pillow on the bed?—but we can show fortitude for one night. Yes, my dear?"

"Yes," Anne replied. Only it did seem odd to share the small room with James. She had, on occasion, shared space with her former companion, Mrs. Jenkinson, or even her maid, Susan. But to share a room with a man!

A husband, she reminded herself, was quite different, though that hardly made it better. Quite common people all shared bedchambers, of course, often husbands, wives, children, and servants together. But a truly civilized couple were not forced to live in such squalor. Anne's mother had told her that she need never concern herself with her husband's rooms. She ought to maintain her own domain, available to her husband when he wished, but in no wise depending on him as if he were a companion. "And the truly refined man will not impose on your solitude often," Lady Catherine had said. "In a well-regulated marriage, the man and woman are as independent states, linked diplomatically but not needlessly entangled. That is how wars, both international and domestic, are begun."

But this was not their house, it was a shabby little inn, and unless Anne wished to share a bed with Nurse, Susan, and Barney, this was the way of it.

James stepped out to give her privacy to ready for bed and returned some minutes later. Anne was changed into her nightdress and gown, face washed and hair in a cap.

"Our host offered to clean and shine my boots," James said, "but my man overheard. He snorted so hard I thought for certain he'd burst a blood vessel and get a nosebleed. I do like a high gloss on my boots, which is well, for I don't think I'd be allowed to choose otherwise." He was already in his stockinged feet and now prepared himself for bed, removing his outer clothing, banking the fire, and suffocating all but two of the candles.

Anne got into the bed, wondering at his sangfroid. Gentlemen were strange!

James snuffed the last two candles and climbed into bed beside her. It was an old-fashioned high bed, so climbing was truly the correct verb. In former times, Anne supposed, children or servants would have slept underneath. As it was, the bed creaked distressingly, and the mattress dipped towards James's significantly greater bulk.

Anne tried to brace herself but rolled half onto him. "Excuse me."

"No matter," James chuckled.

She scooted herself back over, glad he could not see her face in the darkness. The bed was not overly wide, and she could not move far enough away that her arm was not touching his. She turned onto her side, facing away from him. That was better, but now she felt as if she would fall backward as soon as her eyes slipped shut. Also, she began to shiver, though whether it was cold or nerves she was unsure. Anne tried to subdue the shivering, but that only lasted a short while, for soon even her teeth betrayed her with an audible clacking.

James's warm hand rubbed her arm, raising goose-flesh. "I do hope you're not feverish. I should hate for you to be sick over Christmas."

"I do not believe I am," Anne said tightly. Indeed, she did not have the hallmarks that came with her fever: the headache, the tightness of chest, the ache in her legs and back. "I am merely... chilled."

"Well. If you will not hover on the edge of the bed as if waiting to spring out of it, but move toward the middle, that will help." He tugged her closer to himself, and casually draped an arm around her. He was quite warm, but...

"This cannot be proper," Anne protested.

He laughed, which she could feel all through her. "On the contrary, letting my wife shiver through the night would not be proper. Or perhaps proper, but not kind. I often wonder at the disconnect of those two words."

Anne was still stiff, and he sighed. "No, but in truth, Anne, there is nothing wrong with a husband and wife cuddling on a cold night. Milly and I would often share a bed when at home. It is not so shocking."

This did not reassure Anne, but instead made her question the upbringing of his late wife. *Had* she been a true lady?

As if guessing her thoughts, James continued. "Milly was Lord Demeron's youngest; born and bred in London; so, you see I am not as reprehensible as you think me. At any rate, I cannot sleep well knowing you are miserable, so you must accommodate my selfishness." With this, he seemed to be content, and his breath evened out.

Anne did not immediately relax, but slowly her muscles, pleasantly warm after the exhausting days of travel, refused to remain stiff. Lying next to James was not quite like having the most amazing hot-water bottle at her back, or the perfect application of a warming pan...it was both better and worse.

Did well-bred husband and wives truly sleep so? She could not picture her mother lying in such an intimate embrace. Perhaps it was part of the modern manners her mother so deplored.

A new window did not open in Anne's soul that night, but the ivy that obscured several casements was somewhat withered by morning.

{ 9 }

J AMES WAS GLAD TO REACH Pemberley before dark the following day. It was indeed a most stately house and the extensive grounds were enough to inspire enthusiasm in the most lackluster huntsman, which was good, as these house parties tended to feature fox hunts and such.

James would have devoted less acreage to woods and more to the home farm, but well, that was another example of differing preferences. He was quite satisfied to spend a day or two riding to hounds or shooting at stray pheasant. He was not a crack shot but was considered a fair sportsman.

When they arrived, the servants were shown off to their respective rooms and the luggage was unloaded by the very proper footmen of Pemberley. James and Anne were shown into the lower parlor. James supposed it was a very beautiful house, but that sort of thing was not in his line. It was certainly very large. He imagined Darcy must employ upwards of thirty household staff, not to mention the stables and grounds.

In the parlor, Lizzy greeted them warmly. "Thank you for coming all this way for Christmas! Most of our guests are out walking while the light is good, but they should be back at any moment."

She shooed a large white cat out of the chair nearest the fire and brushed it off for Anne. "Please excuse Desdemona, she thinks she is the guest of honor."

James preferred dogs, but he patted the cat when it sniffed his buckskins.

Lizzy hovered a little as Anne seated herself by the fire. "I declare," she laughed. "I cannot shake the feeling that I ought to fetch you another shawl or a better cushion. Which I shall do, but only if it would be helpful."

"No, thank you," Anne said. "You are not my companion and certainly not in a position to wait on me any longer." She looked about her. "Pemberley was never home to a cat."

Lizzy smiled again. "Well, now it is home to two. Georgiana and I both adore them, and since Darcy is still in the first, agreeable phase of marriage where he indulges any outlandish request from me, I cajoled him into it."

Lizzy looked about her as if still bemused that this grand place was her home. "Did you not bring your son with you, Mr. Sutherland? I am sure that Anne said he would accompany you."

"Yes, indeed," James answered, "and very kind in you, for I know not all hostesses welcome bairns. But I know enough not to introduce him to your drawing room; the servants have already shown him and Nurse to your nursery."

"Good, but please do not feel you must stand on ceremony here, at least not when it is only us. One of Darcy's cousins, Lady Honoria, also has twins residing in the nursery, but they are no doubt too young to interest a little boy. I made Lady Honoria's acquaintance in Tunbridge last summer, and she has proven herself quite a friend. Another family with children shall visit soon, as well, so hopefully Barney will have some playfellows for a few days."

"That'll be capital, I'm sure."

"Oh, I hear the walkers returning," Lizzy said. "Let me call them to come in before they go to change."

There were five couples, all of whom seemed connected to the family in some fashion or other. Lizzy performed a round of introductions, excepting only Darcy, Georgiana, and Colonel Fitzwilliam, whom he already knew. The others were strangers, except for the last.

"Mr. Turner, of course," James said, shaking his hand. "How do you do, sir? Didn't expect to see you again so soon. Painting another portrait, what?"

"He's quite a friend of the family now," Lizzy said. "Indeed, Mr. Turner's family is the one that will join us in a few days. But I must not keep you. I'm sure you and Anne will want to freshen up after your long journey."

Anne rested but was still a little tired when the party regathered for supper. The numbers of men and women at the table were even and Anne found herself at Darcy's left hand, opposite Lady Honoria, as befit the ladies of closest relationship and highest rank at the table. Lady Jane, another connection of Darcy's, outranked a mere Mrs. Sutherland, but Anne supposed her own close connection to Darcy had affected the placement.

Even more strange, the gentleman next to Anne was Mr. Turner, the working portraitist. That placement made no sense at all; he ought to have been near the foot of the table. It was, of course, the goal not to have a husband and wife sit together—a good hostess enabled her guests to visit with someone they did not see every day—but there were quite a few other men who deserved a higher position. Sometimes great ladies patronized a favorite artist, though; perhaps Lizzy fancied herself such a patron.

James was seated at the other end of the table, next to Lizzy, who sat properly at the foot of the table, as befit the mistress of the establishment. Anne could not help noticing how much nicer Lizzy's clothes were than they had been in Hunsford. She had better taste than Anne had given her credit for.

James seemed well-pleased with his seat, but Anne was a trifle sorry that he should be too far away to speak with or even listen to. Anne and Darcy never had very much to say to one another; after a brief discussion of the accident on the road, there was nothing else.

Anne's other partner, Mr. Turner, was also quiet. He said everything that was proper on renewing their acquaintance, inquiring into Lady Catherine's well-being and that of Mrs. Collins, whom he'd become acquainted with while painting Anne's portrait. Beyond those topics, his conversation fell away. Indeed, he seemed even less talkative than when she'd known him previously. He rubbed his upper lip repeatedly.

During the dessert course, which Anne forwent except for a little Madeira, Darcy raised his glass. The various conversations at the table quieted, and he cleared his throat.

"Now that our party is complete," he inclined his head briefly toward James, "I have the honor to make an announcement." He cleared his throat. "Mr. John Turner has asked for my consent to offer for Georgiana, and I have agreed. A notice will be in the *Gazette* to-morrow, but we wanted to announce this to our family in person."

A rather intense silence overtook the table. Mr. Turner was a trifle flushed; Georgiana was pale.

"John's family will be visiting on the 26th," Darcy continued, "when we will have an official engagement party for the couple."

Anne's eyes, for some reason, went to her husband rather than to the principals in this drama. Lady Catherine had originally thought *James* an eligible suitor for Georgiana. Was he insulted by this development? Had he known of it? Did he care?

He did not look nearly as surprised as she expected. For it *was* a dreadful alliance. Georgiana Darcy to wed a middle-class painter with no birth, fortune, or family to recommend him? It would be quite as appalling as if Anne herself made such a *mésalliance*.

A flicker of several emotions crossed James's face, but he spoke almost immediately, the first to break the silence. "Many congratulations. I am sure it will be a happy... union." Even he seemed not to know exactly what else to say after. For truly, what was there to say?

Colonel Fitzwilliam followed suit, admitting that he had known of the engagement and offering his own fe-licitations. A low murmur of proper phrases followed, not quite masking the tense feeling that had swept the guests.

Soon the ladies retired from the dining room, leaving the men to their after-dinner drinks. Anne placed herself by Georgiana, all weariness forgotten. "You are truly engaged to Mr. Turner? I cannot help but think... My mother will be most shocked." Anne did not intend to be unkind and would have been surprised if anyone suggested she was being harsh. "Does he... Is his family even genteel?"

Lizzy had hung back in the hallway to speak with the housekeeper, and the other ladies were blatantly listening to this conversation.

"Yes, they are," Georgiana said, in her soft way. Another cat, a calico, was slinking through their ankles and Georgiana scooped it into her lap. "The Turners are very well-educated—the children understand Greek and Latin as well as German and French—and the family is very... kind."

"That is certainly an array of languages," said Lady Honoria. "Is their father... In what occupation is he?" She *did* mean to be kind, but there was no doubt that this was unexpected. Darcy was quite her favorite cousin, and Lizzy was well on the way to becoming her best friend. Lady Honoria had noted the presence of Mr. Turner as a bit of a mystery, but a liaison with Georgiana had not even been in her list of possible explanations. A high stickler was her cousin Darcy! Honoria could not imagine him agreeing to such an unequal match.

Georgiana raised her chin a trifle, still petting the cat somewhat defiantly. "John's father is a teacher and tutor."

"A *tutor*?" echoed Lady Jane. She was married to one of Darcy's cousins on his father's side.

"And John himself is a portraitist," Lady Honoria continued. "What a... fascinating occupation."

"Yes, isn't it?" Lizzy agreed, sweeping back into the room. "A most agreeable gentleman; I think very highly of Mr. Turner."

"She would," Lady Jane said *sotto voce* to Anne, so that no one else could hear. "How the Darcy family sinks. We all know he would have done better to offer for you, as his mother wished."

Anne's brow wrinkled; she did not know how to respond.

"When is the wedding?" Lady Honoria asked, bemused but still trying valiantly to behave as one would at a normal announcement.

"We have not quite decided," Georgiana answered. "Perhaps March."

"Before the Season?" Lady Honoria asked, startled. "I know short engagements are the rule, but I should have thought your brother... Never mind. A spring wedding would be most cheerful."

Georgiana looked uncomfortable, but she did not pretend to misunderstand. "You perhaps thought my brother would insist on presenting me first, on my having a first season still unattached."

"That is generally way of these things," Lady Honoria said candidly, "with a very young lady. Particularly an heiress! But I do not mean to be tiresome. Just because it is generally insisted upon does not mean it is always best. And you are mature for your age, my dear, there is no denying it. I imagine Darcy would hesitate more if he felt this was a giddy impulse."

"Thank you," Georgiana said simply.

"How did you become acquainted?" Lady Jane drawled. "Did he paint you?"

For the first time, Georgiana flushed visibly. "He painted several members of my family over the summer: my two new sisters, myself, and my cousin Anne."

This naturally turned eyes toward Anne.

"Yes, that's correct," she confirmed.

"Was it quite the romance, Mrs. Sutherland?" Lady Jane asked Anne. "Do tell us."

Georgiana looked acutely uncomfortable now.

Anne cocked her head. "Honestly, I did not harbor the least suspicion of this until tonight. Mr. Turner always behaved with circumspection." Even now that

Anne began to rethink their behavior, she could not picture any flirting or indiscretion. "I suppose they did have more conversation than others; Georgiana and Mr. Turner are both interested in religious matters."

This was not at all what Lady Jane had been angling for, and it temporarily stymied her languid inquisition.

Lizzy chimed in, "Yes, Mr. Turner is a Methodist and quite pious. But enough of this, Lady Honoria, will you play for us?"

A quiet musical interlude passed as several ladies displayed their skill. Lady Jane sat herself next to Anne. "I fancy you must feel as I do, Mrs. Sutherland. A *shocking* match, no? And just after Mr. Darcy made his own... well, perhaps not scandalous, but certainly *surprising* choice. How Georgiana is throwing herself away!"

"Perhaps." Anne did not entirely disagree, but she felt it would be disloyal to encourage Lady Jane. When, Anne wondered, had any sense of loyalty to Georgiana taken root in her? Perhaps because Georgiana was the one who had first suggested that Anne might marry James?

With a snap of belated insight, Anne realized that Georgiana had not been quite selfless in directing Anne toward that gentleman. If Georgiana had already had a preference for Mr. Turner, her recommendation took on a rather different light.

Unsure what exactly to make of it, except that she was unsettled, Anne retired early, before the gentlemen came to join the ladies.

{ 10 }

ANNE WAS TIRED, IT WAS TRUE, but not exhausted. At the door of her room, she hesitated and turned away. She continued further in search of the nursery.

By following one dim gallery to the next, she presently came to a short stair that led up a half flight. Here, the sound of wailing aided her discovery.

The mingled golden light of several lamps spilled out from the gap under a white door with flower detailing. Anne knocked once and opened the door. The effect of going from the cold, lonely hall to the bright, loud nursery was quite a contrast.

A large fire burnt in the grate, and it looked as if two new bassinets had been recently added to the room. There were blankets lying here and there, one markedly soiled, which Anne quickly turned her eyes away from. A bottle of milk rested in a pot of water hung over the fire and the smell of warm milk reminded Anne of early memories. An open doorway led to a second room in which Anne could see another nursemaid and another baby. Barney was not immediately visible.

"The babies is well, miss, but they—" A harried nursemaid turned to her and paused. She held a whimpering baby, quite a bit larger than Charlotte's but still definitely in the infant stage. "Beg pardon, ma'am. I thought you was Lady Honoria. You will be Mrs. Sutherland, I make no doubt. Betty! Come collect this cloth at once."

The other nursemaid, holding the second baby and looking none-too-pleased, came out with a laundry pail on her other hip.

"Master Barney has already been put to bed, ma'am," the first continued. "It's the third door along o' the right."

"I suppose it is rather late. I do not wish to wake him."

"Sure and he wouldn't mind a visit from his mum."

Anne went on to Barney's room, thinking that perhaps all nurseries tended toward disorganization, not only the one at Middlefinch.

Nurse was reading Barney a story and paused when she came in.

"Good evening, ma'am. We didn't expect you tonight."

"I was tired of the party. I shall just sit here while you read."

Nurse did read again but rather haltingly and with occasional glances at Anne. "Would you like to read the story for Barney, ma'am?"

"Me? No, I do not read aloud." Although... to read aloud from some adventure tale would not be so taxing. "Another time," Anne amended.

When the chapter was over, Nurse placed a scrap of lace in the well-worn book and set it on a high shelf. She patted Barney's foot. "There now, good night, Master Barney. Nothing to fear in this fine mansion, so I hope you'll try to sleep through the night."

"I never intend *not* to sleep all night," Barney said. "It merely... happens. Did you see the two cats, Nurse? The white one has hair like a lion's mane! Mrs. Darcy said it is called a 'dang Dora,' and the other is a calico."

Anne choked. "It cannot possibly be called... Oh, I believe you mean an *Angora.*"

"Maybe so," Barney said sleepily. He held up a scratched finger. "He doesn't like it if you hold him tight in your lap and rub his hair up like a lion though."

His Nurse snorted. "That's a lesson for you then. Now, that's enough. Say good night to your mum."

"Good night...Anne. I shall call you Anne, as Father does. Is that all right?"

"... Yes, I suppose so." Anne hesitated, not knowing the ritual or immediately remembering one of her own. One instinct bid her pat his hand, another to kiss his forehead. Instead her hand landed on his forehead; she stroked his hair back gently. "Good night, Barney."

Lady Honoria was passing through the dark gallery as Anne made her way back to the bedchambers.

"Why, Mrs. Sutherland, you gave me quite a turn," she said, spying Anne in the dim room. "You are so wraithlike in the darkness. I fancy you are on the same errand as I, to check on your little one."

That put a fine maternal gloss over Anne's visit. Was it true, or had she merely not wanted to go to bed?

"Did you see my twins?" Lady Honoria asked.

"Yes. Your babies are very... large," Anne managed truthfully.

At this, Lady Honoria laughed. "You are becoming a plain-spoken woman, I see. Yes, they are! I shan't keep you. Good night."


James went up to check on Anne when he learned she'd already retired. He was admitted by her maid, Susan, who bobbed a curtsey and withdrew.

"All well, my dear?"

She was wrapped in her dressing gown already, nearly prepared for bed. "Were you aware of Georgiana's engagement? You did not seem as startled as the rest of us were."

James scratched his chin. "I *was* startled that he was here, but once I heard his family was coming, I figured the jig was up."

Anne was faced away from him. She dipped her hands in the ceramic washbasin. "But once you knew he was here... you knew it was for Georgiana."

"Well, yes. I always had a talent for spying that sort of thing. Even at Cambridge I could tell when a chap was pining—usually after the most unsuitable females, too. But honestly, I quite thought Darcy would scotch any little *tendre* she had in that direction."

"I see." Anne dried her hands carefully on a small, flowered hand towel.

"Then there was that ring she kept fiddling with on her hand. Engagement ring, no doubt."

"I did not note...oh, yes, but it was very plain," Anne objected.

"Exactly the sort of thing he would buy. Does her match bother you? He's not what they call a catch, certainly, but it will have very little bearing on our lives. Except perhaps to offer a distraction." He laughed. "We're already attached to a bit of scandal through Lizzy's sister, though Darcy said Wickham's going to be packed off with the regulars to Spain, presently. To which I say good riddance. Now Darcy's young sis is making a stunningly bad marriage; and her one of the richest heiresses in England! I daresay any little talk about us will be quite forgot by the time we get to London." He rocked back on his heels.

"I only wondered whether the engagement bothered *you*. I know my mother's first expectation was that you and Georgiana might make a match of it." Anne finally turned towards him. She spoke rather in a rush. "It is not my business, but since you are a proponent of plain-speaking—and you did me the honor of asking after my feelings in regard to Darcy's marriage—I wondered if this announcement caused any discomfort for you."

"Ah, I see." James finally understood the gist of her questions and felt more comfortable now that she had laid it out. Why could he and Anne not always talk so freely? He sat himself on the daybed by the window. "The situation is not quite parallel—I only courted Miss Darcy for a few months—but I quite see your point. No, the match doesn't bother me in the least. I think Miss Darcy a sweet girl and I think Turner an odd duck but a likeable man. Those are all the feelings I have on the matter."

Anne perched on her own bed. "I suppose if you never offered for her, your expectations were not raised."

James cocked his head. "Matter of fact, did offer for her. Darcy turned me down flat; his sister too young, not yet out, and so on. Didn't think any the worse of him for it."

"And still you came to Netherfield?"

James smiled ruefully. "Never claimed to be a smart man. I'd decided to marry again and hitting the marriage mart in London never appealed to me. Besides, that trip was more than half to help *you*. It was clear your mother was against it, and she is..." He coughed. "Well, she is the sort of woman who ought to be crossed now and again."

Anne frowned, clasping her hands between her knees. "You brought me to Netherfield to... to spite my mother?"

"No, no. Spite is not the right word at all. I have nothing against your mother, a most interesting lady! Some people just have the tendency to rule the roast, you know, like a stud that's allowed to get away with anything. It's not good for a horse, it gets bored and ornery, and it's not good for the stable, people get hurt. Your mother don't know it, but she likes a bit of sass, a bit of push and pull. Witness her interest in Lizzy this summer," James offered as an example.

The emotional complexity of all this was rather more than Anne had expected to digest this evening. She instinctively sensed that he was correct about much of it—her own unpleasant memories of the summer at least partially supported his assertion—but it did not seem right to think of her mother in such terms. Anne shook her head, unable to parse it out. "Thank you for explaining. I am glad that Georgiana's engagement does not rankle."

"Of course." James rose and patted her shoulder. "I can see that you are tired, so I shall retire. Good night, m'dear. I'll just scoot through the door here; I believe my room is adjoining."

He stopped in the doorway. "I enjoy talking to you, Anne, no matter the topic. I hope you will always share what is on your mind."

Anne made a noncommittal noise and he passed on, just latching the door behind him.

Why *had* this troubled her so?

She could come up with no satisfactory explanation except that she had a growing desire to know what James thought about things, even what he *felt* about things. Was that normal for a marriage? She had never much cared what anyone thought or felt until now; people's thoughts and emotions were generally immaterial, were they not?

But James's thoughts—James, who liked to talk and seemed to speak an emotional language quite extraordinary to her—his thoughts were both knowable and material to her life.

LADY JANE WAS A DIFFICULTY. She sat with Anne in the parlor, walked out next to her when the group took a turn in the Pemberley wood, and even rode next to her when Darcy provided carriages to take everyone to church on Christmas morn.

The woman did not like Lizzy, that was clear, but Anne was not overly fond of Lizzy herself, so that couldn't be the full source of the problem. Lady Jane was not critical of Georgiana, though she did bemoan the engagement, which again, Anne could not help agreeing with. And Lady Jane did not invariably speak ill of either lady, but still Anne did not enjoy her company or her comments.

At breakfast: "The new Mrs. Darcy ran downstairs *barefoot,* I saw it myself."

At church: "John's family is no doubt *pious,* but everyone knows that is another word for bourgeois. Probably an odious middle-class family that will forever be pushing into Darcy's circle."

After church: "Do you dislike Christmas services as much as I? Shall we be expected at *evensong* as well?"

Since it was Christmas Day, Barney joined them both for the service and the meal, and Lady Jane did not take much notice of him until he was nearly underfoot as they disembarked from the carriage.

"Careful of your elders," she commanded. "My own boys always allow the adults to exit first."

"Your boys?" Barney asked.

"Yes," she said, with careless pride. "I have three sons at home; the youngest is your age."

"I wish you'd brought them!"

She laughed in a way that made Barney hunch his little shoulders. "They're better off at home; they need to make strides with their tutor during the short break."

This disappointed Barney but he plucked up for the extensive Christmas luncheon Lizzy provide. "Plum pudding!" he exclaimed at dessert.

"Why, yes!" Lizzy said. "It does not rightly seem like Christmas without it."

The adults exchanged presents in the afternoon. Most of the couples exchanged small mundane items. John gave Georgiana a book of sheet music, which made her quite happy. Lizzy gave Darcy an embroidered handkerchief, and he her, a tortoiseshell comb.

Anne presented one gift to James and another to Barney. She rather liked selecting presents.

James's gift was ensconced in a small wooden case, which he opened gingerly. Inside was a glass tube with a small, finely wrought apparatus on the bottom. The whole was filled with a silvery liquid.

"What is it?" Barney asked. "A thermometer?"

"No, better, a mercury barometer!" James exclaimed. He held it up and examined the atmospheric markings, showing Barney how it worked and tipping the tube so that the viscous mercury slid about like living silver. "You see, they have discovered that the weight of the atmosphere varies and can be measured with these instruments. Some are studying how the weather can be predicted by observing a barometer and the variability of wind and temperature. I suspect someday we shall predict storms that are *weeks* away."

Anne dipped her head, smiling. "Your mother said you do not need one; that Old Joseph's bones tell of coming storms in plenty of time, but I thought you would enjoy it since you were talking to me of those experiments about atmospheric pressure and evaporation."

"You were very right! Only now I feel guilty that I bored on about that when you were clearly listening. My mother knows she may think on other things when I become loquacious." He squeezed her hand. "Very thoughtful, thank you."

Barney's present was in a cotton bag, and he quickly loosed the slip cord and opened it.

"It is another dissected map," Anne explained. "This one is the continent of Europe and it was mine as a child. I hope you will like it."

Barney pulled out a piece that was a deep blue with a gilt border running through. "Thank you. I like the colors."

"It was hand-painted in Paris."

"Will you complete it with me? The first time?"

"Oh. Of course, if you like." Anne felt warm and full, and not merely from the meal.

James's present to her was a silver locket of the sort that could hold a lock of hair.

"Thank you," Anne said. She used her fingernail to click it open, but it was empty.

"You don't need my hair," James explained. "Always seemed a daft notion to me—getting hair off people you see every day, when you can just as soon touch the real thing." He brushed his fingers against her hair. "But I thought you might ask Lady Catherine for a lock. I know women miss their mothers, and it would be a nice thing for you. My wife had one for her mother, wore it often."

Anne's lips parted. *But you don't like my mother,* she nearly said. But that did not matter to him, he had thought of what *Anne* might value. "Thank you. That is an excellent idea."

Anne clasped the locket around her neck.

Barney was taken back upstairs by Nurse, with promises that he should enjoy some playmates on the morrow.

James left her side, eager to show off his new instrument to Colonel Fitzwilliam, who seemed to have more interest in such things than the other gentlemen. Lady Jane soon joined Anne.

"Mrs. Darcy kissed her husband just now—Twice! Shameless! Before us all!" Lady Jane shook her head. "Tomorrow shall bring worse, I am sure."

"I doubt she will kiss the Turners," Anne replied dryly.

Lady Jane trilled a laugh. "You are too comical."

When James escorted Anne up the grand staircase later that night, but before the rest of the party retired, she asked him, "Why do we like some people and not others? Assuming neither has done anything hurtful or wrong?"

"Don't know that I have adequate philosophy for that one. Or perhaps that would be anthropology—study of man, what?"

"But you... you understand people better than I."

"Hm. Name a soul and I'll give you my honest opinion of them, but natural law isn't my line."

"I don't know if I ought, but... the person is Lady Jane. I cannot be comfortable with her."

"'Course not," James said at once. "I wouldn't like you so well if you could cozy up to that vindictive viper. Her husband is the same; not sure who infected whom, but they are two of a kind. I haven't heard either utter a word that wasn't better left unsaid since we arrived. You know the adage, 'If you cannot improve the silence...' Well, they do not."

"Her comments *are* rather critical."

"Exactly. Slaughtering cattle is far easier than raising them."

"Sorry?"

"Never mind. In my opinion, there are two courses with such people, either avoid them—that is generally my choice—or answer with such unrelieved cheeriness and optimism that *they* avoid *you*."

Anne smiled. "You might do that, but I do not know that I could."

"Try it then. Experimentation is not just for strains of beets and barometric devices, you know. There is nothing to say you cannot try an experiment with a person such as her. In fact, house parties such as this are the perfect occasion." Anne saw that he wanted to make her laugh, for he grew more ridiculous. "What shall I try? Perhaps I shall answer with a color every time Lady

Jane's husband makes a snide criticism. Umber. Saffron. Crimson. He already thinks me a halfwit."

Anne shook her head, though her smile grew. "You would sound mad."

"No, I should couch it in such terms as to put him in no doubt of my agreement. 'Crimson, sir, I concur.' 'Yes, saffron to the $n^{th}$ degree.' 'Fine umber for a Darcy!'" James waggled his eyebrows meaningfully.

Finally, Anne laughed. "You are absurd."

"Yes, but a little absurdity is the spice of life."

"I do not think many would agree."

James had reached her door and entered with her. "But I did not say which spice. Good night again, m'dear. I hope you have absurd dreams." He kissed her and used the connecting door to his own room. "Thank you for talking to me."

Susan looked on with wide eyes. "Did Master have much to drink?"

"I don't think so." Anne reconsidered. "Maybe."

"Don't often see him so jovial." Susan began to undo the pearl-seed buttons on Anne's sleeves. "Though Timothy says as how Mr. Sutherland always has a funny word for the men and a ready laugh for their pranks."

"He does like to talk and jest. I suppose he likes when people talk *to* him as well." James had said something similar a few nights ago. "His form of affection, perhaps."

{ 12 }

Lizzy was not blind or indifferent to the awkwardness of inviting the Turner family to Pemberley, but she and Darcy had decided it to be for the best. Georgiana had impulsively invited them when she stayed at their home for a few nights. After a brief but intense discussion, another, more formal invitation had been sent.

Several of Darcy's family were not taking the engagement well, namely Lady Jane and her husband, but Darcy had decided, in the manner of a rider heading for a jump composed of both timber and water, that it was best to take the leap at a gallop. Full force.

And so, on December 26, midday, John's family arrived in their carriages. Lizzy had offered to hire one for them—it was difficult to know what gifts were appropriate and what offensive!—but John had assured her that his father's carriage was perfectly capable of making the journey. His elder sisters would come with their husbands in their own carriages.

Lizzy had given particular orders that the Turners were not to be delivered to the parlor all at once, as might normally be done in such cases, but shown to the library where she, Darcy, John, and Georgiana could greet them privately. Georgiana had spent several days at the Turners' home in November, and Darcy had gone to retrieve her and to make their acquaintance, but Lizzy had not yet met them.

Lizzy was not apprehensive on her own account, but on theirs. If there were only her own feelings to consider, all would be easy. But Georgiana was sensitive and John's unknown family... well, those pushed above their normal rank did not always display to the best advantage. For example, there was Charlotte's father, who could not stop speaking of his knighthood by King James, or Lizzy's own mother, who had frankly married above herself and never acquired the manners to go with it.

Georgiana had said only glowing things about the Turners, but that was all Lizzy expected of her. Georgiana was rather like her sister Jane in that way.

It was quite a crowd that was presently brought into Pemberley's stately, holly-bedecked library. Ten persons, counting the baby! Lizzy expected the infant but was slightly taken aback to note that one of John's sisters was quite far along in pregnancy. Lizzy was far from offended, but surprised that the lady would travel five or six hours from home when she looked as if she might be lying in at any moment!

They all greeted Lizzy quite cordially and the awkwardness she had feared did not at first appear. A fire made the room warm and a hearty tea made it welcoming. The younger members were hungry after traveling so many hours, and they sat down to a merry tea.

Lizzy sat next to Mrs. Turner, the matron of the family, who asked her civil questions about her enjoyment of the neighborhood.

"You have not been married long, I think?" Mrs. Turner added.

One of John's middle sisters, a pretty, dark-haired girl named Martha, who was about Georgiana's age, spoke up timidly. "Georgiana told me it was a great romance."

Lizzy laughed, "Well, perhaps it was, but a rather bumpy one. And no, ma'am, we are not long married, only since late summer. This is my first Christmas with the Darcy family. But if I had known the quantity of presents and foodstuffs I should be allowed to buy for presents, I should have accepted him much sooner." Lizzy caught Darcy's eye and laughed at his long-suffering look.

"Providing treats for servants and tenants, you mean?" clarified Mrs. Turner. "I am sure that is good of you."

"Not good *of* me, ma'am, but good for me! At home, of course, we did the same, but we only had three servants in the house and a handful at the farm; I quite enjoyed the challenge this year."

Mrs. Turner's eyes opened a little at this information of Lizzy's relatively humble origins, which Lizzy hoped would set her more at ease. As for the rest, well, it would be foolish to pretend that there was not a great disparity in wealth, but Lizzy felt that morbidly avoiding any conversation that touched on their situations would create unnecessary walls.

Georgiana interposed quietly, "I was so glad to relinquish that duty to Lizzy."

"We always make cinnamon-clove pomanders for Papa's students," John's youngest sister, Ruthie, said. "And this year one of the students gave Papa a copy of Niebuhr's *Roman History*."

Darcy inclined his head. "I have been meaning to obtain a copy for my own perusal."

"Yes, in fact I brought it with me," that gentleman said, "in case I should have time for reading. Niebuhr is quite the authority on the subject."

His wife was giving him a significant look, and Lizzy nearly laughed aloud when he said innocently, "What, my dear? Oh, ought I to offer it on loan to Mr. Darcy? But not until I have finished it, surely?"

Mrs. Turner turned a dull red, but Darcy waved a hand. "I should be happy to borrow it when you have finished, but there is no rush, sir."

The youngest Turner, a boy of twelve named Silas, had finished a large helping of cake, several scones, and ham. He was very proper, but Lizzy thought he was only refraining from fidgeting restlessly in his seat by sheer willpower.

"Silas, I hope you will not mind, but I have half-promised a little boy who is staying here that you would play with him. He is stuck in the nursery with Lady Honoria's twins and would welcome a little manly company."

"I should not mind, ma'am," Silas said properly. He hesitated only a second, before adding eagerly, "I should quite like to skip rocks on that smooth lake we came past; I could take the little boy."

"I'm sure he could be persuaded, but perhaps we should check with his nurse."

"I can accompany him to the nursery," Ruthie offered.

Lizzy smiled. "I see what it is and suspect that you would beat your brother at skipping rocks if at all possible. Yes, quite. I shall ring and have you both shown to the nursery. I'm sure one of the footmen can accompany you to make sure Barney does not fall in."

In the event, it was James who accompanied a group of young people to the Pemberley lake. He spotted the youngsters headed to the nursery and knowing it would be a treat for Barney, he offered his company at once.

He thought of asking Anne if she would like to come, but a brisk wind blew, and he suspected she would decline. It was not frigid however, so once Barney and the other two children were well-wrapped in coats, mittens, and caps they were on their way.

"This is a huge house," Silas said as they descended to the front door. "I should not like to sweep it."

"Do you often get stuck with the sweeping?" James asked him.

"Yes. Bessie, our girl-of-all-work, will do it sometimes, but on laundry days, baking days, and Thursdays it is usually me."

"It is a large house," Barney agreed. "I must not run off as I do at home, for otherwise I should get lost and die of starvation."

James barked a laugh. "Nurse's warning, I take it."

Barney nodded.

"It would take longer than that to die of starvation," Silas said. "Now, thirst, that would do you in a couple days. And I read that explorers must drink much more as they attain higher altitudes, otherwise they sicken quickly. The lower pressure combined with exertion saps the natural moisture of their bodies."

"Ugh, why must they go to such horrible places?" Ruthie asked. "I'm sure no one asked them to."

"That is not the point—" Silas started.

"Do you want to be an explorer, then?" James interrupted good-naturedly. "First to the South Pole, perhaps?"

"No," Silas said decidedly. "I want to be a scientist. A chemist, in particular, but I daresay I should need a thorough grounding in minerology, biology, and physics to begin."

"And mathematics, do not forget."

Silas's straight young shoulders slumped. "Yes, sir. That, too."

Barney patted the bigger boy's arm. "That is how I feel about porridge without raisins."

Ruthie and Silas laughed.

"Yes," Ruthie said, "Silas must eat his raisin-less porridge every day, and to make it worse, Father encourages him to stop mathematics at any time and devote himself to history and languages."

"Isn't that good?" James asked. "Not many fathers would allow you to stop with arithmetic."

"No, it isn't good," Silas explained. "I am already well beyond arithmetic, I am studying trigonometry, and when I am hating it, I cannot say, 'Father insists on this and thus I obey.' I must make myself do it!"

James laughed rather harder at this, but apologized. "I believe your father to be a very wise parent. For when you are a man, obedience to fatherly authority passes away, but force of will remains."

He inquired more particularly into Silas's interests and was pleasantly surprised to find that the boy was knowledgeable as well as ambitious. James even mentioned the medicine and water that they were trying for Anne, and Silas immediately entered into the mystery of it. From the particular efficacies of iron and other minerals on the body's humors they moved to the exact grams that might be useful "based on mass, you know, sir," and even further to the possible benefits of powders versus solutions for various treatments.

At the lake, Silas's intellect was put aside in favor of competition, though he was disappointed not to find more smooth stones. However, he gamely shared those he did find with Barney and Ruthie. Barney's stones were *chucked* more than *skimmed,* but the little boy delighted in his father's and Silas's better throws. Ruthie too, had an arm on her, and what with one thing and another, James passed a pleasant afternoon.

{ 13 }

ANNE WAS RESTING IN THE CORNER of the drawing room when Lizzy and Darcy brought the Turner family to be introduced. Lizzy's cat, the Angora named Desdemona, of all unlikely names, lay curled in her lap. The cat had found, on experimentation, that Anne remained more still than the others and did not pet so aggressively as to make it impossible to nap. Anne could not forbear stroking the cat, but very lightly. She enjoyed the warmth and rumble of the cat's sleepy purr though it seemed decadent to spend an afternoon thus. She could not quite silence Lady Catherine's animadversion on the perversity and uncanny independence of felines, but many ladies of high *ton* enjoyed cats, and so Anne silenced her doubts.

Pemberley had several drawing rooms, and this was the largest, but it began to feel small as the crowd of Turners entered. If Anne had expected them to feel abashed or cowed in the face of such unaccustomed luxury, she was disappointed. They were not uncouth, but they were a loud and happy bunch.

Lady Jane positioned herself by Anne's chair, occasionally stooping to make observations in her ear. This stopped when Lizzy presented one of John's sisters to them, a stout young matron named Maisie. Lady Jane's gaze fixated on the alarming size of this lady's midsection; Anne did not have to guess what she was thinking.

"What a beautiful puss," Maisie said. "I quite adore cats."

"Yes, she's lovely." Whether it was Anne's own perversity, or the influence of James's suggestions, Anne wasn't sure, but she did not follow that innocuous lead, choosing instead to defy Lady Jane's critical gaze. "I believe congratulations are in order, ma'am. I was recently at a christening for my dear friend Mrs. Collins. What a joyous occasion."

"Yes, thank you. I hope it will be." Maisie beamed.

Lady Jane smirked. "How brave of you to be out and about so late into your time."

She chuckled and patted her stomach. "I daresay I ought to have stayed home, but I was eager to meet Georgiana's family. I couldn't bear to be the only one left behind for their engagement party."

"And yet we were not given any choice," Lady Jane said coldly.

At this, Maisie raised a brow. "Ah. I see my husband was right; he always is."

"How so?" Lady Jane drawled.

Maisie smiled. "Just let me assure you that we shall not come dirty to dinner or accost you in London as old friends. Indeed, after this short interlude, we shall be as strangers."

This direct address seemed to discompose Lady Jane slightly. "Yes," she said uncertainly.

Anne, with the first burgeoning of what in later life would be good hostess instincts, made a slight motion to Lady Honoria.

"Have you yet been introduced yet?" Anne made Maisie known to her. "Lady Honoria's twins have been sharing the nursery with my new son, Barney."

"Twins?" Maisie exclaimed. "What a chance. I have been wondering if I may in fact be carrying twins, for I am sure there is a battle occurring within me. And you see I am as large as a barn, and me only seven months!"

Lady Jane wrinkled her nose at this indelicate talk and moved off, but Lady Honoria did not look offended at all. She weighed Maisie with her eyes. "It is possible, but tell me..." And they began a discussion that even Anne, in the midst of her desire to spike Lady Jane's guns, could not listen to without becoming queasy.

She placed the cat gently on the chair and joined Colonel Fitzwilliam, who was the best known to her in the party other than Darcy.

"Well, Anne, how do you do?" he said. "You're looking fairly hearty this Christmas season."

"Yes, far better than normal. Colonel, are you happy with Georgiana's engagement?"

He turned a surprised look on her. "No commonplaces at all? That's not like you."

Anne warmed her hands above the fire. "I like to know things, I find. I like to know what people are thinking."

In return for her forthright answer, Colonel Fitzwilliam quietly admitted, "As it happens, I couldn't have been more shocked at Darcy's acquiescence. I rather think he was bludgeoned into it by the happenings on his wedding day... But mum for that."

"Indeed."

"They seem like affable people," Colonel Fitzwilliam continued. "I had begun to suspect that Georgiana would always dislike the London scene, and that she would never make a grand match. I have nothing against this family in particular, but there is no doubt it will cause a deal of talk." He shrugged. "But you though, Anne. Mr. Sutherland! Quite a catch, everyone agrees. A excellent choice, even if he was all to pieces."

Anne froze. *All to pieces? As in, financially ruined?*

She did not have time to inquire more, for Lizzy, who was still circling the room making introductions and rearranging the small groups to the greatest felicity—as well as generally trying to snuff any flames before they grew—brought another sister to them.

"Fitz, Anne! This is Miss Martha Turner. May I present my cousins though marriage, Colonel Richard Fitzwilliam and Mrs. Anne Sutherland?"

Martha curtseyed and smiled.

Anne's mind was still miles away—all to *pieces*?—and so Colonel Fitzwilliam made good-humored conversation with the girl. He was less surprised by Anne's quiet than by her previous directness. Anne barely registered any of it.

But when Colonel Fitzwilliam went to refresh his tea, the girl, Martha, leaned toward her. "I say, Mrs. Sutherland, are you feeling quite the thing? Perhaps the fire scorches you? You look...quite unhappy. Let me help you to this nice lounge where you may recline."

Anne accepted, for a great lassitude enveloped her, making it hard to walk and think. She felt as if her heart had slowed, that her blood was congealing by sheer force of gravity.

A cup of tea was presently pressed into her hand and Anne brought it to her lips from habit. Was it true that James was in dire need of funds when he married her? Such reverses of fortune happened, of course, and in such cases, gentlemen often married an heiress or rich tradesman's daughter to bring themselves about. It was common.

But James?

The only thing Anne knew was that she could not stay in this loud, bright, bustling room any longer. "Do you think...you could call my maid?" Anne whispered to Martha.

Martha looked about for a bell pull or a servant but did not immediately see one. "Well, I will inform Mrs. Darcy—"

"No, I do not wish to make a scene." There would be exclamations, pity, questions—even if brief, it would not do. "Would you escort me to my room?"

Martha took Anne's arm and unobtrusively accompanied her out. Martha was the most romantic of her family, her eyes often dreamy and unfocused, but she was also practical and kind-hearted. If her secret heart thrilled at being allowed to see more of the house, if her creative spark imagined a story behind Anne's sudden indisposition, none of that influenced her behavior.

She escorted Mrs. Sutherland quietly, sensing the lady did not want to speak. In her room, Martha pulled the cord and they waited quietly for the maid. "Do you have a companion or someone else I can send for? Your husband?"

Anne shivered and pulled a shawl from the foot of her fancy bed. "No, thank you. There is no one else."

{ 14 }

ANNE WENT TO BED, CLAIMING a headache, which Susan had every reason to believe. She had never yet attended her mistress in emotional distress rather than physical.

Anne did not sleep. She knew that James would come to check on her before supper when he came to dress, or just after.

She wanted to ask him for the truth.

She did not want to ask him for the truth.

Why should it even matter? Such marriages were common. They were *sensible*. She did not even want her marriage to be a love-match, for those were willful displays of foolishness by such people as Lizzy and Georgiana. Anne had never expected to marry for love, but she had thought—perhaps—that she and James had married for friendship.

But he had not even proposed to her; if anything, Anne had proposed to *him*. It had been an arrangement—an alliance—amicable but not emotional.

As Anne lay on her side, cold feet tucked up as far they could go, she felt again James's arm around her the night they'd spent in that hovel of an inn. She had thought him... affectionate. She had thought him...warm. Kind. Friendly.

But he was all to pieces, and Anne was a well-heeled young lady. She was not the heiress Georgiana was, but not so far off. In addition, Anne would inherit Rosings Park, which was a considerable estate. If James was in difficulties, marriage to her would offer immediate relief in both tangible assets and new lines of credit with his bankers.

It was prudent of him, if so.

But Anne pictured again the letter she had seen by accident, which had precipitated a whole new direction in her life. It detailed how her former companion, Mrs. Jenkinson, "could not wait to get away from the oppression of Rosings," "unrelieved by Miss de Bourgh's sullen, ungrateful air." How Mrs. Jenkinson "longed for the cheerful company of real friends."

Real friends. When Mrs. Jenkinson had been Anne's only friend for so long.

James came before dinner. He entered very softly for a man his size, unlatching their communicating door with stealthy precision and tiptoeing to the bed.

Her eyes flickered upward to him.

"Oh, you are awake." He put his hand to his heart. "Startled me. I thought you must be sleeping." He perched on the edge of her bed. "I have been out to the lake with Barney and the youngest two Turners. That Silas is quite a bright lad. Shouldn't be surprised if he makes a name for himself someday. But how are you faring? Not feeling quite the thing, eh?"

"No." Anne said simply.

"I'm sorry to hear that." He rubbed her arm gently and pulled her hand into his. "Your fingers are like ice." He rubbed them, smoothing his warm, strong fingers over hers, between them. "I'll call Susan to build up your fire. What else can I get for you?"

Anne pulled her hand away. She could not bear it. "I am fine, but I cannot come for supper. Please make my excuses to Lizzy and the others."

James's brow furrowed. "As you wish, of course. Until tomorrow, Anne."

He came to check on her again after supper, but Anne pretended to be asleep.

Darcy was taking a moment alone in his study the next day—confounded house parties! People everywhere!—when Anne sought him out. He was drinking a snifter of brandy despite that it was before noon. If only all these people could be gone, and it could be him and Lizzy again. How he had enjoyed the fall; their quiet family party was exactly what suited him.

When he saw that it was Anne who had knocked, he raised the narrow-stemmed glass and tossed it off. "Good morning, Anne. Lizzy was sorry you were not feeling well yesterday."

In truth, Darcy felt this was an example of Lizzy's generosity. Darcy himself suspected Anne was just as disapproving of the Turners as Lady Jane, and that Anne had purposefully absented herself from the meal to make a point.

He had never received a tongue-lashing from Anne, she was generally quiet, but he thought perhaps he was to receive one now. Or would she dissolve into tears and ask him what her mother would think of this company? He had never seen her dissolve into tears or hysterics, but he had seen her faint multiple times and so felt it was well within her capabilities. Between the two options, he would prefer anger.

To his surprise, Anne said nothing about the Turners. "When you and my mother prepared the settlements for my marriage, what were they?"

Darcy wondered if he would need more brandy. "I do not recall the particulars at this exact moment, but the gist of it is what you would expect. Your funds and income in interest transferred to him. His primary estate is entailed on Barney, but any further children of yours are to receive the Kent estate, the second one in Surrey, and so on. The dower house is to be at your disposal until your death or remarriage. Rosings Park is to remain your inheritance, so you may also remove there in your later years if James is gone... the usual things, cousin."

Anne did not look satisfied. "I do not know what the usual things are. Is James... Were his affairs... in order?" She stumbled over the words.

"In order? The entail and trusts, you mean? His lawyer and mine went over it all..."

"Was he all to pieces?" Anne blurted.

Darcy wished Lizzy were here. "No, I wouldn't quite say that. He'd lost a tidy sum in an unlucky investment a few years ago, which lead to a mortgage against Middlefinch. Then his experimental farm cost more than he expected to start up, which exacerbated the problem. But it is sufficient to its own expense now, and he will pay off the debt by and by. His mother..." Darcy trailed off. James had been quite forthright, but Darcy wasn't sure he ought to share that lady's indiscretions with her new daughter. Sowing discord in a family was none of his design.

"Her horses?" Anne guessed. "Tell me."

Darcy sighed. "She spends too much on her stable, but the real trouble seems to be that she gambles far too freely at the races. But she is hardly the only gentle-woman to do so."

"So, he was... in difficulties."

"It was prudent for him to marry," Darcy agreed. "You must not think he was in any way mean about it. He agreed to every protection for you and your inheritance. It's true that he was in difficulty, but far less than many a peer, and through less fault of his own."

"And you didn't think to tell me?"

Darcy reached for the brandy and poured himself another inch. "If he had been in difficulties due to his own immoral lifestyle, gambling, or other vices, I certainly should have done my best to discourage the match. Yes, I would have told you the whole. But as it was... honestly, cousin, I thought the fact he was dangling after Georgiana would have enlightened you as to his motives. I heard him say in your company that he needed to re-marry. Why else did you think he was hanging out for a wife?"


Anne looked away. She had thought it was because James was a gregarious man who liked conversation. She had thought he wanted a friend because he was the sort of person who enjoyed companionship, and after he mourned his wife, was ready to try again.

But now it sounded so simple and obvious. James had not been hiding it from her; he probably thought his comments about needing a wife were perfectly clear.

But now Darcy was frowning. "Has there been some difficulty? You are supposed to be receiving an allowance. Has he withheld it?"

"No. I receive it quarterly."

"And it is adequate to your needs?"

"Yes."

"Then I do not perfectly understand. Is there some other financial entanglement that worries you? Do you fear he is running into debt in some other way?"

"No, I doubt it. Though his mother did buy another expensive horse."

"Unwise, but it will not ruin him," Darcy assured her.

"Of course not," Anne said helplessly. "His creditors are no doubt far more accommodating since he wed. Please excuse me."

Anne went straight back to her room. She was being a coward, but she had never grappled with such a feeling of disappointment.

Perhaps her heart had grown stronger along with her body, for her emotions, which before lived demurely in a corner of her soul, were now as loud and problematic as the Turners were boisterous.

JAMES MIGHT HAVE NOTICED Anne's aloofness more if he hadn't been distracted by the influx of Turners. It felt like a quite a large house party now, which was just what he liked. There was always someone to walk about with, enjoy a game of billiards or chess, and have a glass of wine.

Pemberley had a kingly wine cellar, and their butler could be trusted to select and decant properly. The Pemberley butler was a distinguished personage indeed, too proper to display the least weakness, though occasionally a haunted expression overtook him, particularly when he set down an '89 Burgundy and picked up a pitcher of water to serve John and his father. The riches of Pemberley had never been thus rejected. The Turners did not partake in the drinking, of course; as they were all strict Methodist abstainers.

Then there were the children. The nursery now held three babes plus Barney, and frequently Silas and Ruthie, who at twelve and thirteen, were not particularly interested in sitting quietly with the adults all evening.

Pemberley was a fine place for youngsters, however. Darcy made them free of the stables where a pony and several mares were put at their disposal. A fishing expedition was also attempted, though less successfully. A damp wind came up, which quite cut through their clothing, and though Darcy did manage to land a very small bass—which he allowed Silas and Barney to pull in and disentangle—this got the boys' hands so cold and red that even they were ready to retreat after a mere three hours.

Anne had recovered from her indisposition and joined the ladies for most of their activities, which put James's mind at ease.

Upon returning from another visit to the stables with the children, he snagged the elder Mr. Turner for a rematch at chess, which they set out in the corner of the drawing room.

Tonight was the engagement party, for which they would need to dress presently, but there was always time for a quick game.


Anne was feeling foolish for indulging such a stormy reaction to the unexpected revelation. She was determined to resume the festivities as if nothing had happened. For truly, it had not. She merely had a better understanding of her marriage and the circumstances attendant upon it.

She could not help eyeing James's game of chess in the corner and feeling inexplicably sad that he had not asked her to play. But why wouldn't he prefer a knowledgeable competitor instead of one who could barely challenge him?

Martha, the sister who had escorted her to her room, sat nearby with a novel open upon her lap. She mouthed the words silently as she read, and Lady Jane had just done an exaggerated mimicry of this for Anne's benefit.

"Is your novel interesting?" Anne asked, rather than responding to this.

Martha looked up. It seemed to take her eyes a moment to readjust to the indoor light, as though she had been on a sunny plain or windswept mountain aerie only moments before. "Oh, yes, ma'am. Papa does not often allow us to read novels at home; there are better uses of our study time. However, I could not bring my lesson books here, so I am quite enjoying it."

"Do you enjoy writing as well as reading?" Anne asked.

Martha sighed gustily. "I only make up stories in my mind; the work of putting characters down in ink, stroke for stroke, causes me to lose the thread."

Lady Jane yawned and stretched her neck this way and that. "Anne, have you read *Count Brougham's Mis-*

*tress?* The author captured so many witty caricatures! Prinny, Duke Marsden, Lady Marsden and her *chère amie,* Henry Gould... It is delicious."

Martha looked away.

Lady Jane laughed lightly. "Ought I to apologize? Did I violate some middle-class taboo?"

Martha squared her shoulders. "We are taught that adultery is not less than a sinful betrayal of both man and God."

Lady Jane's voice was condescending. "Very right you should feel that way. Proper morality for the masses."

"James's uncle is a writer," Anne offered, to turn the conversation. "He writes gothic tales of horror."

Lady Jane yawned again. "I truly have grown weary of black veils and dripping caves."

"Do you mean *The Mysteries of Udolpho?*" Martha exclaimed. "I have wanted to read it."

"I believe Obie's latest is not fantastical in that way," Anne explained, "but rather an exploration of mad science, evil automatons, and such."

Martha sighed happily. "I do love a frightening story. *The Iliad* and *The Odyssey* are quite adventurous, also, but Papa will not let me read them in the original; he says it is not fitting."

Anne asked. "Are you still studying with your younger sister—Ruthie, is it?"

"No, ma'am," Martha said, on her dignity. "I am seventeen and I help Mama run the household, now that both my sisters are married. Furthermore, Papa says I may advertise as a governess in the spring."

"A governess?" For a moment, Anne had forgotten what class of person she was speaking with. "Of course."

"Mama had suggested," Martha looked around shyly, "that I might ask a recommendation from Georgiana, or Mrs. Darcy, or one of the other ladies present. It should help ever so much."

"Riveting as the selection process for a governess may be," Lady Jane said, "I am growing weary. I need a diversion. Shall we play a game of whist, Anne? I'm sure two more would oblige us. Do you prefer high or low stakes? I do not care, I am sure, only we must wager *something* or it is incurably dull."

"I don't play well," Anne said, rather thankfully. "I barely know the rules." Lady Catherine had generally excused Anne from such games.

Martha went back to her book.

"Besides," Anne pointed out, "I do not think we have time for more than a hand or two before we must dress for the party. I believe I shall visit Barney, since he will be kept out of the way tonight."

Martha hopped up. "May I accompany you to the nursery?"

It was when James saw Anne and Martha leaving the parlor together that he had another good idea.

"I say," he asked Mr. Turner. "That daughter of yours, Martha, did Ruthie not tell me she will be out for governess soon?"

Mr. Turner did not pull his eyes away from his pieces. "Why, yes."

"Well, how about if she were a companion instead? Anne is not always well, and she has no one but her maid at Middlefinch. Good, solid girl, Susan, but not a comforting sort."

Mr. Turner looked a bit vague, his mind still on knights and pawns. "Perhaps. That is... I suppose if she did not..."

Mrs. Turner, who was embroidering a new handkerchief for her youngest, nearly choked at this lackluster response. She leaned forward. "I beg your pardon, Mr. Sutherland, but I overheard your conversation and must beg to reply. Martha would be honored to be Mrs. Sutherland's companion. I have feared she might be too young, a trifle too easy in nature to be a successful governess—though she is a hard-working, obedient girl!—but a few years of further experience in the world would be excellent. In short, if Mrs. Sutherland is amenable, I know Martha would not hesitate."

"Excellent!"

Mr. Turner moved his queen. "Checkmate, sir, I believe."

His wife elbowed him.

"What, my dear? Oh, yes, thank you for the offer, sir. Much thanks. But checkmate all the same."

Mrs. Turner pinched the bridge of her nose.

{ 16 }

John brought Georgiana's hand to his lips. She already wore the simple engagement ring he'd given her, and the happiness with which she twisted it to and fro made him grin like an idiot.

He could hardly believe that they were still to marry, even after she had faced down the mixed response among her extended family. He'd trusted in her faithfulness, but he would not have blamed her if the actuality caused her some doubts.

"I do not know why we had to have an official engagement party, much less a ball," Georgiana murmured. "None of your family even dance. Are you certain your father is not offended?"

John tucked her arm around his as they stood at the edge of the Pemberley ballroom. It was still decorated in Christmas greens and silver bells, quite beautiful. A number of neighborhood families had joined them, which, along with the persons staying at Pemberley, made upwards of twenty-five couples: more than an adequate number of guests for a ball held at a country estate.

"No, my father is fine, I discussed this with him already. It is not his preference, perhaps, but he understands that your family are of a different world than his. And Mr. Darcy assured him that no one should pressure any of us to dance."

Martha caught his words and slumped a bit. She was standing demurely but interestedly next to their mother, looking as if she would have been very happy to have learnt.

"Besides," John added, "my mother, who is generally the stricter of the two, assured him that it was necessary to set us off on the right foot, to make sure that we occasion as little gossip as possible."

"I suppose so," Georgiana said. "But I should not care so much about gossip."

"Never fear," said John, "the party will be over soon, and you may retreat to your room and cuddle your new cat."

Georgiana smiled. "Lizzy is a miracle worker; as soon as I told her of your mother's cat and how much I should love to have one when we are married, she said, 'Why wait?' I cannot think how she convinced Darcy to allow it. And not just one but *two* cats."

"I can hazard a guess," John said knowingly.

Georgiana blushed.

"I d-did not mean—" John stammered. "Only that your brother has looked so happy of late, that I shouldn't think it took more than a simple pout on her part."

Maisie approached them then, looking rather red in the face. One hand hovered near her abdomen. "I say, John, I should not like to make a scene, but I am not feeling quite right. Could you fetch my husband to me? I've lost Thomas somewhere."

John blanched. "Good heavens, Maisie. Are you...?"

"I do not know for certain." She involuntarily clenched one hand into a fist in her skirts. "But if you could *fetch Thomas*, that would be excellent."

Georgiana fluttered as John left them to work his way around the dance floor. "What should we do? The doctor, of course. Do you have an accoucheur? Or no, you would not, I suppose. Our Lambton doctor is excellent, I assure you."

Maisie breathed out slowly. "I am not overly concerned. I helped attend Sally, you know, and I remember when Mama was lying in with Silas. He took nearly two days, though usually later children come faster than firsts."

Georgiana swallowed. She herself had no experience with childbirth. "Let me escort you into the anteroom, at least," Georgiana offered. "You cannot like standing about like this."

"No, no!" Maisie exclaimed. "You of all people cannot leave the room, Georgiana. This ball is for you. I should hope not to make any commotion. Thomas will escort me to my room, and he will have the butler send a boy for the doctor. You do not even need to say anything to your brother if you please." Maisie looked a little embarrassed. "Honestly, it is my own fault. Thomas urged me to remain at home with him. You probably think I have no decorum, but I am aware that I was rather too far along to come into company."

"I am glad you came," Georgiana said stoutly. "Only... I do hope you will be well! You cannot have a baby in secret. Surely I must tell my brother?"

"No, please, not yet. John shall tell my mother and I shall be well. If you feel you must enlist further advice, perhaps Lady Honoria? She seems very kind."

Thomas and John appeared from the parlor which had been set up as a smoking and card room, and Maisie was whisked away without further ado.

"I cannot possibly stay at this party and pretend there is not a lady giving birth upstairs," Georgiana whispered to John. "Can you?"

He tugged at his collar. "I think we must do our best. Lizzy has gone to such pains; shouldn't you hate to disappoint her?"

The evening was interminable to Georgiana. She did her utmost to appear as normal, after discreetly informing Lady Honoria of the event, but somehow the news inevitably spread. First there was Lady Honoria's husband, Chuff, who needed to be informed why his wife had disappeared. Then it was John's sisters, who quickly realized Maisie and their mother were missing.

James, after dancing with Anne and several other ladies, brought Georgiana a glass of punch. "Allow me to wish you happy, dear girl. I am honestly glad things have come together as they have, and I hope that you will be as happy with John as I am with Anne."

Georgiana thanked him distractedly, wondering if the footman who just approached Lizzy was telling her about Maisie.

James chuckled. "I gather the disappearance of half the Turners means that another party is taking place above stairs."

Georgiana looked at him with wide eyes.

"I am not so dim-witted as I look," he said. "Keep a stiff upper lip. Another hour and the guests will begin to drive home before the moonlight is gone."

He drifted back to Anne, who looked alarmed after he bent over and whispered in her ear. Like an invisible mist, the news seemed to be spreading to the whole room.

But Darcy approached her with a smile, seemingly untroubled. "I know you are nearly Methodist already, but do me the honor of a last dance, Georgiana."

"Of course."

He quirked an eyebrow at her as they joined the lines. "Is there some reason I learned from my *valet,* rather than a member of my family, that one of my guests is lying in at this very moment?"

Georgiana bit her lip and circled in the dance, coming back to him presently. "Maisie didn't want to make a fuss. She felt badly at disrupting our celebration."

"Yes, and I am so volatile I cannot be trusted to be discreet, is that it?"

"Of course not!"

When they came together again, he said, "That being said, perhaps we ought not tell Lizzy yet. I wouldn't want her to worry."

Colonel Fitzwilliam also danced with her. "Cannot believe I am dancing at your engagement party, Georgie. Makes me feel old. How can I be a guardian of such a grown lady?"

"You won't be my guardian for much longer," Georgiana said boldly, "you will be fancy-free again."

He squeezed her hand. "I am happy that you are happy. Mind you, I don't think you ever would have gotten your painter without Lizzy's help."

"No, I know I shouldn't have," Georgiana agreed. "She changed everything."

"Well, I hope you will be content with your choice. Soon it will be you bringing little Turners into the world, like that gal who disappeared several hours ago, eh?"

Georgiana huffed. "Does everyone know what is happening? Perhaps we should have made an announcement."

"Don't know. Daresay it don't matter whether it's known or not." He tweaked her chin.

Georgiana was avid with repressed curiosity by the time the last carriage had been brought around to the house and the last guests carefully tucked into their furs.

Lizzy and Georgiana lingered in the front hall to say goodbye, and when the front door finally shut, thankfully cutting off the frosty night air, Lizzy put a hand to her brow.

"*That* was difficult. I forgive my mama for every attack of nerves she suffered after hosting such a crowd. But of course, *she* was not nervously straining her ears for the wheels of the doctor's gig or listening in dread for sounds of pain drifting down the stairs."

"We tried so hard not to worry you," Georgiana cried. "You told me it was important that the ball be described as 'Pemberley's finest.'"

"And you did your job admirably, though you are no actress. But I saw for myself Maisie's red face and abrupt departure. I am, if I do not sound too odiously like Miss Caroline Bingley, credited with *some* quickness of wit."

Georgiana pressed hands to her warm cheeks. "I am glad it is over."

"As am I," Lizzy agreed emphatically. "I do hope this was my trial by fire and not all Pemberley occasions will be so fraught with undercurrents. Now I shall go get rid of Lady Jane and the others. Hopefully they will be exhausted and head to their beds at once."

{ 17 }

GEORGIANA RAN UPSTAIRS AND CAUGHT Mrs. Turner stepping out of Maisie's room. "How is she? Does she need anything?"

Mrs. Turner wiped her forehead and patted Georgiana's bare arm. "Not at the moment, my dear, the servants are doing all we need. Hot water, cloths, and so on. The doctor does not want her to eat or drink at all, and I quite agree. I think she has still some hours to go."

"You are satisfied with the doctor?"

"Yes, completely." Mrs. Turner turned a little pink. "I think he... he does not realize that we are not quite the normal guests of Pemberley. He is treating us with *every* consideration."

It made Georgiana a little sad that this was such an unexpected thing for Mrs. Turner. "As well he should," she said. "For you are not guests, you are family."

Mrs. Turner's tears welled up and ran down her roughened cheeks. "Goodness gracious, I never weep, I am just that beside myself. I wouldn't have had this happen in your home for a thousand wishes, but thank you, Georgiana." She squeezed the young girl tight then mopped her eyes. "I must go tell Thomas how she fares, and I better not be napping my bib or he'll think Maisie in danger."

"What should I do?"

"There is really nothing... you may as well go to bed..."

At Georgiana's incredulous look, Mrs. Turner wavered. "At least, do change out of your ball gown. Sally is assisting me, but I daresay Martha and Ruthie might appreciate some company in their room."

James escorted Anne up the stairs to bed. Neither of them spoke until they reached her room; the silence pressed on him and he could not help straining his ears for any clues.

"Don't hear a bloody—sorry, blasted sound." He held Anne's door for her, still listening. "Perhaps she is like Barney's mother; she was a quiet one as well. Didn't cry out until the very end." He shuddered. "It's no easy thing waiting and waiting during such a dangerous time. I do not envy that Thomas fellow. I think I lost a stone of weight from sheer anxiety."

Anne moved to her looking glass, carefully unclasping her earrings and necklace.

James shut the door behind them. "What's more, our doctor treated me like a perfect imbecile, as though I had not night-calved far more than any haughty London gentleman! But there, I daresay I should've worried Milly, so perhaps it was for the best they kept me away."

Anne was now removing her hair pins. Usually Susan would do that, James realized. No doubt the upset in the house had discomposed the normal arrangements.

"All well, Anne?" James asked. "You're very quiet."

"Did childbirth weaken her? Milly, your wife, I mean?"

"Weaken her? Well, for a bit it did, and no mistake. Birthing is a challenging occupation. But the illness that took her off, that began later. Recurrent fevers, bloody cough..." He shook his head, not wanting to think of it. Nor was he being exactly comforting. "That Turner girl will be fine, though. She looks hale and hearty."

"I hope so, for Georgiana's sake as well as her own. This will be what she remembers of her engagement party."

"That's so, I suppose. Much more exciting than the average. Do you mind that we hadn't a grand party for our engagement?"

"No. I do not have a wide acquaintance; there was no need."

"No need, perhaps, but ladies enjoy a fine affair like this. We shall host a splendid ball when we rent our house in London."

"Would that be prudent?" Anne asked. "Considering the state of our finances?"

James didn't need to ponder. "Of course! I budgeted for such things from the outset, knowing you would want to go for the Season since you were never presented in the regular way. I promised you we should go, didn't I?"

His entire lack of self-consciousness confirmed what Anne had thought. He had indeed not meant to deceive her, but he had assumed her more observant and worldly than she was.

"Yes. Good night, James," Anne said.

He put his hands in his pockets. "Not sure I can sleep with this wretched, tense silence in the house. Might go keep Thomas company." He kissed her cheek as he always did before taking his leave.

Anne pulled the cord and Susan appeared soon, breathless and a bit guilty. "Apologies, ma'am, I was in the kitchens. There is such a to-do. The housekeeper says as there hasn't been a baby born here since Miss Georgiana and they hadn't planned on such a thing. And then one of the ladies' maids says as how that Turner family shouldn't'ta come, and didn't the housekeeper give her a trimming! Sent her off with a flea in her ear about speaking against Mr. Darcy and dispersed the lot of them."

Susan readied Anne for bed at once, but over an hour later Anne was still lying awake, though it had to be nearly two in the morning. She could not stand another moment of suspense.

Wrapping her dressing gown tightly around herself, she ventured first to Georgiana's room. There was no answer, which left Anne at a loss. She could certainly not join James and the gentleman waiting in the library or wherever they were. She did not want to knock on Lizzy's door; they were not friends.

She heard girlish voices not far away, however, and feeling very stupid but determined, made her way toward them. She scratched softly at that door; it was one of the rooms allotted to the Turners. She would merely ask if there was any news and go back to bed.

The door opened to reveal not just the two Turner girls, but Georgiana, Lizzy, and Lady Honoria as well.

Anne was surprised to see them all, but not more than any of them were to see her.

Lizzy rose at once. "Did our voices disturb you? I thought we were being so quiet, too!"

"No," Anne said. "I... wanted news of Maisie. How is she?"

Lizzy's eyebrows rose. "She is as well as can be expected. She is attended by the doctor, her mother, and elder sister, and they say there is no undue reason for worry."

"Thank you." Anne remembered that they were not friends. "I shall go—"

Lizzy interrupted her quizzically. "Would you like to join us? We are just being silly girls in here, passing the time as best we can, but there is room on Ruthie's bed for another."

"I—Yes, please."

Anne's presence at first silenced the cheerfulness of the group, for cheerful they were, although the occasion was serious. The peculiarity of staying up all night with other females had made the older ladies feel young and the young ones feel older.

After a moment, Lady Honoria picked up the thread of their conversation, and by asking Anne after the details of the christening in Hunsford, she was eventually included.

It was a strange night. The room was cozy and full, with quite the most female atmosphere Anne had ever felt. It was their own special space.

Anne found herself grateful to be included, and for someone who had been taught from childhood to pity others less "fortunate" than herself—which was no way

to learn humility or gratitude—it was quite a novel sensation.

{ 18 }

Mrs. Turner counted five clangs of the hall clock as the baby was being rubbed and wrapped. When she was satisfied all was well, she put the ladies out of their suspense.

"Maisie is fine as can be; though time will tell. And there were not twins after all, but one fine, strong girl. Sally declared her to be the next Boadicea, so queenly and proud she looks already."

There was much hugging and some wiping of tears. Mrs. Turner did not feel entirely comfortable embracing their fancy hosts, except Georgiana, of course, but she noticed happy clasps between Anne, Lizzy, and Lady Honoria as well.

Satisfied that all was in hand, Lizzy insisted that Mrs. Turner and Sally and the others should rest at once, so that they might not be worn down before they were needed again. She herself could take the first watch with

Maisie and the new baby, along with Lady Honoria's nurse, who had gotten a good night's sleep.

Mrs. Turner at first resisted this, but being an experienced woman, realized that she was being a zany. She ought to accept what benefit she could from having a helpful hostess and house full of servants and nursemaids. Truly, this might be the easiest grandchild she would help deliver! She did not even have to soak the birthing cloths to keep the blood from setting before she could get to the washing, for they had been whisked away nearly at once. Lizzy had assured her that the laundry maid would get a little extra for helping in that way, and that Mrs. Turner was not to think of it.

She hesitated to leave Maisie, but her daughter was sleeping, as well she ought, and Lady Honoria's nursemaid promised to wake her if anything should go awry. Thomas had been allowed to hold his infant daughter and had gone to seek his rest also.

Weary with care but satisfied, she slept.

Anne awoke in the mid-afternoon with the odd hollowness that came from a confused stomach and missed meals.

Many of the guests were taking their leave that day. The Turners had planned to do so as well, but circumstances would obviously delay them. Lizzy had a simple buffet set out in the breakfast parlor, so that her guests might eat when they chose or when they awoke.

Lady Jane was already in her traveling dress when she entered the breakfast parlor and met Anne, who had just selected two savory scones to accompany her tea.

"Ah, you are awake at last! Thank heavens. The house has been a veritable tomb. I am just come to have a morsel before we depart."

"We were up very late," Anne explained.

"I know! It almost makes me pity Mrs. Darcy to have such guests. I do not pretend to regret anything I shall leave here except your society, Anne. We have made it bearable for each other, have we not? Your husband tells me I shall see you in London in the spring, and I shall look forward to renewing our acquaintance. You really must have me to Middlefinch after the Season, you know; then we should have so much to discuss. I know we should see eye to eye on everything."

Anne fingered a crumb off her lip. "I do not know... You would find Middlefinch sadly flat, I fear. It is not like Pemberley."

Lady Jane tittered. "If by that, you mean not overrun by tutors and tradespeople, I can only be thankful."

"I cannot even promise that," Anne said vaguely. "As Georgiana and John may come for a visit." This was not a lie; they *could* come for a visit, although there were no plans to do so. In fact, as Anne thought of it, she realized that she might enjoy such an interlude.

Lady Jane's husband soon came to escort her to the carriage, and Anne was not sorry to see her go.

James poked his head in some minutes later. "That bracket-faced lady gone for good?"

Recognizing Lady Jane from this description, Anne assented.

"Excellent." His eyes looked rather heavy and blood-shot, though cheerful. "I have the devil of a head from last night and can't bear her complaints." He poured himself a cup of tea and looked rather wistfully at the beef.

"What is amiss?" Anne asked.

"Well, nothing, strictly speaking. Only there we were, wishing Thomas happy, and I may have had a drop too many. Colonel Fitzwilliam and I both like a good brandy, and Darcy has *very* good brandy. And the Turners drink naught, which meant all the more for us." He took in her expression. "Don't worry, I seldom over-indulge! Very dull dog I am, in general."

"I'm sure it's none of my business."

"Here's something which *is* your business. That girl, Martha. Don't seem superstitious and ain't a watering pot. Got it all fixed up."

Anne could not make much of this. "Perhaps I am still tired. *What* is fixed up?"

"Martha! A new companion for you. Her ma says as how she's happy to do so."

Anne opened her mouth to object but shut it indecisively. She still did not relish the idea of a companion, but as girls went, Martha was unobjectionable. Last night in Martha's room had been one of the most curiously happy nights of Anne's life. The salary, however, would change things, would it not? Money always changed things.

"No need to poker up about it," James said, as if he could read her mind. "She was looking to hire herself out regardless, why shouldn't she work for you? Doin' her a favor."

Anne slowly nodded. "Perhaps. I must speak to her about it."

Martha clasped her hands and dipped a small curtsey in sheer excitement. "Yes, ma'am! I *should* like to be your companion." She could not believe her good fortune. A fine house! In the south! Perhaps Martha should get to visit the seaside or even one of the watering places. And London! Was it gauche to say she would give anything to see London at the height of the Season with Mrs. Sutherland? Worse, was it *sinful* to feel that way?

Slightly damped, but perhaps that was just as well since it prevented stammering or unconsidered exclamations, Martha nodded once, seriously. "I would be honored to take that position in your household. I hope I should suit."

"It may be dull for you," Anne said. "I am not a lively person and I am often unwell."

"All the better," Martha said blithely. Then she blanched. "I mean that I am terribly *sorry* you should be unwell, but that being what it is, I would rather be a *needed* companion than an *unneeded* one." She hoped desperately that Anne was not already offended. "Also, I should not mind helping with Barney, as he gets bigger. Your nurse is already past the time she can be running up and down stairs and chasing after him on a pony."

"Perhaps. Lastly, I should not like to live with someone who... who dislikes me," Anne said plainly. "If that comes to be the case, we should have to reconsider the position."

Martha blinked. "But I do like you. Why would I not? Georgiana told us you were quiet but brave, and I saw exactly what she meant with Lady Jane."

Anne furrowed her brow. "Those would be satisfying descriptors, if true, but my life does not call for much bravery."

"Perhaps more than you think," Martha said.

"Yes, well... I suppose we have only to coordinate when you may begin and the logistics of conveying you to Middlefinch."

But James, upon application, had no idea of waiting. "She'll come along with us, of course. Her family can ship her a trunk in due time."

"I did bring several warm outfits with me," Martha put in, "plus my nicest things for the ball."

"Exactly," James said. "She's got the needful and they can send the rest."

"I suppose," Anne agreed, "but Mrs. Turner may not be prepared to lose her so quickly."

"Mama will not mind," Martha assured them.

{ 19 }

THEIR PARTY WAS MUCH DIMINISHED that night, for the guests were gone and the Turners had retired early. Anne and Lizzy went to the parlor alone after dinner.

Lizzy sat in her usual spot, and her cat jumped up to sit purring at her side. Lizzy stroked her absently. An open book lay on the side table, which Lizzy had no doubt been reading that afternoon. She looked...at home here. Every bit as if she belonged to Pemberley, and Pemberley to her.

"I am happy for you," Anne said.

Lizzy looked inquiringly at her.

Anne looked away uncomfortably. "I know my mother made you aware that she expected Darcy to offer for me. We have never discussed it, but you might be glad to know that I am happy for you, and for myself. Things are better as they are."

Lizzy, for once, did not look at all as if she wanted to laugh. "Thank you, Anne. I should be pleased to count you as a friend."

Anne wasn't sure that was exactly what she'd meant, but... she was willing to accept it.

"So, what should we do with the evening?" Lizzy looked a little longingly at her book. "Music? Reading?"

Anne could not pretend to be a great reader like Lizzy. And music was nonsensical, as neither she nor Lizzy were particularly musical. Although, to be fair, Lizzy could play the pianoforte far better than Anne. The thought caused her to pause. She had never before thought of their musical accomplishments in such a way. Lady Catherine always qualified Lizzy's playing with her deficiencies, but even a deficient player was superior to one who had never tried.

The chess set nearby still showed the final move in James's last game. "Would you care to play chess?" Anne asked Lizzy.

"Oh, certainly," Lizzy agreed, again surprised. "But I warn you I learned to play with my father, and now I play against Darcy! I am not bad."

Anne began placing the pieces back into their starting position. "Then you will probably win, though James says that I am fast improving. But I will never grow proficient if I do not practice."

Lizzy reset the white pieces, then moved a pawn forward. "You sound very like Lady Catherine," she commented cheerfully. "I believe she told me the exact same."

Anne rubbed her thumbnail across the crenellations of the rook. "I wish she had said so more often to me. I was ill, but..." Anne trailed off.

But what? Her mother had made every allowance for Anne. Where was the fault in that?

Perhaps it was that her mother had seen nothing *but* Anne's illness. Yes, that was the problem. It was not Lady Catherine's fault, but she had never encouraged Anne to be anything *other* than a young lady defined by illness.

Lizzy moved her knight. "I think that marriage agrees with you," she said gently. "You seem happier."

Anne pursed her lips. "Life is, in some sense, a skill to be learnt, is it not? And although I may always be deficient, I should rather play than not."

When the time came for the Middlefinch crowd to leave, Martha was hard-pressed to keep her excitement within bounds. She had said that her mother would not mind losing her, and as far as evidence went, she was correct. Whether this was strictly true or not, or whether her mother did suffer some pangs at abruptly parting with her middle daughter, was stringently concealed by

Mrs. Turner, who presented none but a serene face as they said their goodbyes the following morning.

Ruthie, who might be considered the next to be pitied, both for affectionate connection to her older sister and the inevitable increase in her responsibilities, was pragmatic. "I shall miss you, but now *I* shall be the one to help Mama, and that means I shall leave the schoolroom!"

Martha laughed. "You might at least pretend to regret losing me."

Silas sighed and hugged his sister. "You must ask if I can visit Middlefinch; I should like to inspect Mr. Sutherland's experimental farm."

She pinched him. "I am a *companion*; I can't go inviting people to their house."

He pinched her in return. "Sure you can. I would."

Martha bid the rest of her family goodbye with the blithe excitement of one who had never been separated from her family for even one night. Soon the Middlefinch party was on the road.

Barney looked back at the house as long as it was in sight, then turned to sit correctly with a sigh. "That was a jolly house. I wish I had a brother."

Martha sat across from him, next to Anne. "Perhaps you will someday."

Barney frowned and then looked at Anne with gathering excitement. "That is a good idea. Will you have a baby, like Silas's big sister? Then I should have a brother, which I quite think I ought to have." He pondered. "But you needn't have twins, like Lady Honoria. They were rather *much.*"

James cleared his throat. "Don't plague your mama for a brother, lad. If it happens, it happens."

Martha felt Anne grow tense and realized she had committed a faux pas. Everyone knew the upper class was strange about marriage and children, which to Martha's family were quite commonplace things.

"I'm sorry, I didn't mean... Barney, do you know your alphabet?" she said brightly. "Let us find things out the window that begin with vowels."

{ 20 }

THEY REACHED MIDDLEFINCH in the midafternoon of the third day, having made better time traveling south than they did heading north. The overcast sky had offered little light into the carriage all day, and Barney had grown sleepy barely four miles before they reached Middlefinch. His head rested against Martha's arm, and she rubbed his shoulder to wake him, for of course he had dropped to sleep just before they arrived.

"You're home, Barney."

Martha rubbed her own eyes as well. She could not possibly be *tired*—she'd barely moved for three days!—but her body felt lazy and lethargic.

Middlefinch was not so grand as Pemberley, but it was still a fine large house. The warm peach color of the front façade was a welcome sight in the midst of the dreary day. The windows, however, were mostly dark, except for the two nearest the front door.

When Timothy hopped down from the front bench and opened the carriage door, a blast of chilly, salty air dashed into the closed box of the carriage. Anne gasped and wrapped a shawl around her head and mouth. Barney grumbled sleepily. But Martha, being a hearty northern girl, felt a welcoming surge of energy.

She leapt lightly down, flashing a smile at Timothy. They'd gotten pretty well acquainted at Pemberley, as Silas and Barney had wanted to ride the pony nearly every day, and Timothy had accompanied them whenever James wasn't at hand. Susan and the other servants had just arrived before them, and Susan looked rather angrily at Martha.

Barney and James alighted next, and Martha waited to offer her support to Anne. At least, that is what she planned to do, based on the brief advice her mother had been able to give her. But James offered Anne his arm, and she of course took it.

What exactly did the companion of a married lady *do* when the husband was present? There truly ought to be an instruction manual. Perhaps she could find one in the library.

Martha dropped back. "What a lovely home you have, Barney."

He huddled in his little jacket at the bottom of the shallow steps to the front door. "It has six bedrooms and a gas stove," he said proudly, but with a shiver. His pride did not prevent him running up the steps and slipping first into the warm hall when the door was opened by a smart footman.

A large fireplace on the right hand of the great hall cast welcome heat. Anne however, stumbled and clutched at Mr. Sutherland. He put an arm around her waist, holding her up.

"Anne, are you well?"

Her head seemed to roll, as if too heavy for her neck. Martha hovered uncertainly on Anne's other side, hands out. "Can I— Should I—"

"I feel faint," Anne whispered. "I think I must lie down."

Mr. Sutherland took a wider stance and swept Anne up in his arms, carrying her near his chest. "I'll have you in your bed in a trifle, my dear. Just lay your head on my chest and close your eyes."

Martha followed behind them up the stairs. Although Anne had explained that she was often unwell, Martha had not given it terribly much thought. Anne had seemed fine at Pemberley, but now...! Shouldn't Anne have a nurse or a doctor nearby, rather than a young, ignorant companion?

On the stairs they passed an older man, quite alarmingly disheveled. His waistcoat hung loose on his thin, stooped frame, he wore no collar, and his graying hair looked quite wild. James merely said, "Excuse us, Obie."

Martha offered a quick nod and half bob. One could not curtsey properly with one foot on the next stair.

Then there was a fine lady in a riding dress with plaited auburn hair.

James adjusted his grip. "Just nip ahead and pull down her bed, would you, Mother? Anne is feeling faint."

Martha followed them in, but Susan, who had arrived in the servants' carriage, shooed her away.

"I'll do all that's needed, Martha, I'm sure." Susan fluttered her hands. "It's my job to undress the mistress and make her comfortable. Do you go on."

The door slammed shut in Martha's face.

She stepped back. Well and what was she to do next? She did not know what room would have been designated for her. Indeed, neither Anne nor James would have had time to write of her coming, so no arrangements *could* have been made yet.

So then... was Martha to go back down to the hall and find Barney? Then there was that strange man on the stairs. Ought she to wait here? But it was rather chilly. A fine, bracing wind was one thing when one was out of doors, but to stand alone and forgotten in a chilly nook of the house was less energizing.

But she was an adult now, properly employed. She must act like it, and not like an uncertain little waif waiting to be led by the hand.

Having bolstered her confidence, Martha went resolutely down the stairs to search for the housekeeper and consult with that lady. For Martha, though dreamy, was not unacquainted with pluck.

Anne's vision had narrowed quite alarmingly as her body transitioned first into the cold wind and then into the heat of the house. Carriage rides never agreed with her, and perforce she had eaten little in the last few days. It seemed to have caught up with her. Her body felt both light and heavy. So light as to not know which way was down, but so heavy as to have no power of resisting the pull of the tilting floor.

James laid her in her own bed, and Anne scarcely knew who else was in the room. A quick open and shut of her eyes merely confirmed it was her own snug bed she was being put into. She heard Susan's murmurs and James's worried tones.

Exerting herself, Anne mumbled, "I will be well in a few days. A cool cloth for my head, Susan." The smell of ammonia and thick sweetness reached her, and she held up a hand. "No, not the *sal volatile* I received at Christmas. I do not need reviving, I need rest."

A broad, warm hand covered hers. "I think you must eat, my dear, you haven't had more than a few bites of toast since Derbyshire."

Anne grimaced, but knew he was right. "Broth, then."

A lady's quickly stifled snort made Anne open her eyes once more. Lady Beatrice's mouth was pressed thin, and James looked at her sharply.

"I will tell the cook," she said. "He probably ought to have expected it."

"Probably," James said shortly. "Go on, Mother, I'll join you soon."

James still held her hand, but Anne slipped hers away. "You needn't stay here. Susan will see to me. I am too tired to keep my eyes open."

James was not so confident in his role of bedside attendant as to push past this blatant dismissal, but he would have been perfectly content to wait at Anne's side. Sighing heavily and thinking once again that he really would *not* allow Anne to go on any more taxing journeys for at least a twelve-month, James took his leave.

Nurse seemed to have swept Barney off to the nursery—probably for tea-time—so James joined Obie and his mother for his own belated tea.

He gave them the news from their visit, but with a distracted gaze. He could not help but wonder whether this exhaustion might send Anne into a prolonged bout of ill health. Was there more he could do to strengthen his wife?

"Speaking of which," James interrupted his own thoughts and looked to his mother, "you seemed nearly cross with Anne when she requested broth."

"Cross?" She sipped her tea. "No, but... Anne is... Never mind. I ordered the broth, did I not?"

"Cut line, Mother."

Obie coughed uncomfortably and fixed his eyes vaguely on the ceiling.

She sighed sharply. "It really is moot, only... I wish you had consulted me before you offered for Anne! A perfectly acceptable girl in her way, only she is such a... such a crib-biter."

James, accustomed as he was to his mother's tendency to fall back on horse analogies when she was at a loss, was not as shocked as he might have been, but he was not happy.

"That is most unfair." A crib-biter was a horse that bit and pulled at its stall or manger, looking as if it were trying in vain to swallow large hunks of wood. They arched their necks and strained and made a queer grunting as their throats contracted. It often caused colic. "Nor do I have the least idea what you mean."

"I only mean that...it is so hard to train horses out of such behavior! Such a useless habit and causes all sorts of problems, besides being senseless, even for a horse. I steer clear of them myself. Incurable windsuckers... You understand, I'm sure."

"Afraid I don't," James said, voice cold. "It is not Anne's fault she is ill and so easily knocked up. Her mother says she has been ill since childhood."

"Yes, but... Anne makes no effort! She sits by the fire or lies on her bed or reclines in the parlor. It wouldn't do anyone any good. She says she likes horses, but she has not once stepped foot in the stables, though I have invited her. She might visit the village or take a turn about the grounds. But she will do nothing! I fear no amount of water or pills will make her well, with that lassitude of spirit."

James generally viewed his mother with a tolerant eye, but now his brows drew together. "Not every woman has your robust constitution. Do you think it was Milly's fault she sickened and died after Barney was born? Ought to have gone walking, had she?"

His mother blanched. "No, Milly was not at all like Anne. Her death was tragically unfortunate, but even the strongest can be brought low by disease."

"And in my view, even the strongest can be brought low by a disorder they've had since childhood. The truth is you have judged Anne to be lazy, but I do not think you are correct."

His mother spread her hands. "I don't want to argue with you. You are tired from your trip."

James sighed. "I am at that."

Obie suddenly sat up straight. "What's more, only thoroughbreds."

Lady Beatrice pressed a hand over her eyes. "We weren't truly speaking of horses, Obie dear. Finish your tea, love."

He set his mouth mulishly. "Crib-biters. They are always thoroughbreds. I like Anne."

James's mouth quirked at this somewhat elliptical compliment. It was true that the malady mainly affected thoroughbred horses, not your run of the mill cob, and he supposed that was Obie's way of complimenting Anne. At least he had remembered her name.

"She is indeed a thoroughbred," James agreed.

Obie suddenly shrank in on himself.

"What's amiss now?" Lady Beatrice asked him.

"Pretty girl. In the hall," he whispered.

James looked over his shoulder. Martha stood nervously in the doorway.

"Your housekeeper had me put my things in the blue bedroom," Martha explained, "just above Anne's. She said I might still have tea."

James sprang up. "Blast if I did not forget you entirely! Do come in."

He introduced her, though Obie's reply was nearly inaudible because he was so shy of strangers. In fact, James could not remember the last time Obie would have met a stranger. The family was lucky he had taken to Anne as well as he had.

Lady Beatrice held out her hand. "You look like a strong, sensible girl. Perhaps you will do Anne good."

James sat and threw back the rest of his tea. He just wanted Anne to be happy. And perhaps Anne did look lazy or indolent to the casual observer, but he suspected that was not her personality, merely her situation. Dash it, there was more to her than her affliction. He caught glimpses of it.

Of course, many ladies of society *did* seem to enjoy the importance of illness; they might just as well be introduced as Lady Megrim or Duchess Decline so much did their conversation and identity cling to their ill health. But if James had anything to say about it, Anne would get to choose whether that became her fate.

{ 21 }

By the time February blew into Kent, the household had achieved a new equilibrium, and Anne, though wavering almost weekly from fever to cough to health and back again, did not dislike the new normal. Between Martha, Barney, Lady Beatrice, and Obie, not to mention James, she had far more company than she had ever had at Rosings Park.

Despite a few bad spells, she passed a healthier January and February than she had for many a year. She could not say that the new course of water and powders (a new concoction that James had requested from Dr. Blackburn) had healed her. She seemed to catch infection about as often as she did before; however, it seemed each trifling cold was thrown off faster. Instead of turning into an inflammation of the lung, she had good spells between each reoccurrence.

James's occasional comments on finances, mortgages, and other costs—comments, she realized, which he had made all along, only she had not noticed before being rudely awakened—*did* remind her unpleasantly of the circumstances of their marriage, but she strove to put it out of her head. If she withdrew slightly from him, it was entirely internal and nothing he could be aware of. If she also disliked knowing that her new position in life, from her companion to her new family, her husband to her home, were only a result of money—needed and provided—well, she could also put that out of her head. Where had these foolish, plebian notions of untainted affection and friendship even come from?

"I think I shall ride today," Anne told Martha, on the twenty-eighth of the month. The clouds had blown off leaving an enticingly blue, sunny sky. Martha looked up from the manuscript she was clutching anxiously, one of Obie's old stories which she had enticed him to give her. Obie, Anne thought, would do nearly anything Martha asked of him, having got beyond his initial shyness, but not beyond a sort of helpless bashfulness in her presence.

"A ride?" Martha repeated, no doubt shaking her attention free from ghouls, vampires, or other horrors. "That's a splendid idea! I took the liberty of asking Mama if I might have Maisie's old habit, so I am prepared."

Anne sent a footman to the stables with a message for the grooms to prepare two horses, and she really felt rather excited by the time Susan had helped her into her long-skirted riding gown. If she indulged in the hyperbole that Obie's characters were prone to, she might say that it had been an *eternity* since she had ridden, and she missed it.

East of the house, but before the hops field, there were several outbuildings. The old barn, the new barn, a long, narrow stable, the grooms' quarters, and two small smoke houses. Part of the Middlefinch woods approached the new barn, and Anne heard birdsong beyond the normal lowing from the cows.

In the stables, clean sawdust, leather, and manure gave off their familiar scents and Anne breathed deeply, happily. Old Joseph did not seem to be anywhere about, but at the end of the stable, they found Timothy and James saddling up four horses.

James looked their way with a warm smile. "I was just returning when your message was brought! How could you dream of riding around Middlefinch for the first time without me?"

Anne did not know quite what to say; it had not occurred to her to tell him. Thankfully the question was rhetorical, for James continued.

"Beautiful afternoon! I thought we might ride over to Little Funtam, our creek, and circle back through the farm. I'd love to take you as far as the village, Forefinch, but I don't want to overtire you on your first excursion."

Anne had no fault to find with this plan and mounted neatly with James's help. Martha yelped a little as Timothy tossed her into the saddle and Anne raised an eyebrow. "Martha, you do ride, do you not?"

"Yes, ma'am," Martha said, struggling to arrange her leg over the pommel and to tighten the overgirth strap which held her leg in place. "But we generally just use a block to mount." She looked reproachfully at Timothy, who grinned.

James eyed her. "You rode that fat pony all over Pemberley, but I suppose I'd not given your prior experience much thought. Timothy, keep an eye on Martha and Marybelle."

Anne got the reins expertly in the correct hand and held the top pommel with the other. "I shall be sore tonight, but I am glad to be riding again."

"That's the ticket," James said, heaving himself onto his horse.

They were off and Anne enjoyed the feeling of freedom and power that came with the height and joy of riding a fine horse.

"That's Lettybeth you're riding there," James told her. "My mother picked the names."

"Lettybeth and Marybelle were not your inventions?" Anne asked seriously.

James opened his mouth, but then saw her smile. An answering mirth grew in his eyes. "Full of sass, are we? I shall have to watch you."

He led them north of the house through the open woodland, describing some of the good hunting he had. During a pause, Martha said, "I have just realized, Forefinch and Middlefinch comes from the Latin *forefenges,* meaning a protective skirting of wood. Which means there must be a relic or ruin somewhere nearby that the wood skirts."

James nodded. "More than one, the Normans built several fortifications, though I confess I'm not sure which went with the naming of our wood.

When they reached the creek, the land dropped away about ten feet where the rushing water overflowed its banks.

"Little Funtam," James said, as proudly as if it were his own invention. "It flows into the Stour River further on, and I've never once seen it completely dry, even in the hottest July. But now let's turn to our left and come around that way."

Crossing through James's fields, which he was already busy seeding with experimental additives and so on, Anne was disposed to be pleased. At least if she *was* married for her fortune, her husband was spending the money on something real, not gambling or debauchery or cards. Her mother did not approve—her letters had, if anything, only grown more critical of James in the last few months—but absence was causing Lady Catherine's voice to fade somewhat.

Anne was also pleased when they saw Lady Beatrice. She was trotting around a practice ring, watched carefully by Old Joseph on his horse, but she pulled up when she neared them.

"Well! Anne! On a horse. Will wonders never cease."

"Have I not told you I enjoy riding?" Anne said. She was not so blind as to have been unaware that Lady Beatrice did not believe her.

"Quite. I am glad James convinced you to give our poor beasts a try."

"They are anything but poor beasts, Mother." A muscle twitched in James's jaw. "And Anne decided on her own to ride today."

"To be sure," Lady Beatrice said. "And Martha, I am glad to see you out of the house as well. You must be feeling stifled after these months indoors."

"I am always thankful to go out in spring. Mercifully, here there is no snow!" Martha said blithely. "Last winter we barely stirred out from October to March. *Cito transit gloria mundi.*"

Lady Beatrice looked startled, but Anne was becoming accustomed to Martha's excursions into Latin.

"It's a beautiful day," Martha said, more circumspectly.

"Yes, but that sounds just as well in English," Lady Beatrice said. "Bluestocking or not."

"Yes, ma'am."

Anne felt surprisingly defensive. Yes, Martha was a bluestocking, a girl so versed in education and languages as to be at times a trifle tedious, but... she was *Anne's* companion, not Lady Beatrice's.

"*Gloria mundi*, indeed," Anne said, wondering what her mother would say if she could hear her.

James smiled tightly. "We really must continue on our small tour. Until supper, Mother."

22

MARTHA AND TIMOTHY FELL BEHIND again as they went on.

"You talk a lot of Latin for a female," Timothy said. He was tall and good-looking, save for his front two crooked teeth, though she hardly noticed those anymore.

"A woman can learn Latin just as well as a man," Martha said roundly. "Sometimes better." But recollecting that Timothy was not, in fact, one of her brothers, and had probably never studied a lick of Latin, her posture relaxed a bit. "Not that it is so very useful for a companion. But when I am a governess, it will be helpful if I can prepare the boys for school."

"Why'd you want to be a governess?" he asked. "Don't seem likely."

"I'd rather be a governess than a laundrymaid," Martha said. "I like children and I happen to be rather a dab at languages. Furthermore, I can send half the wages to my family.'

"Ah."

"Where is your family? Do they live in the village?"

"Aye. I'm the youngest. My father was lucky to apprentice me to Old Joseph. They're getting on in years, and my older brother was pressed."

"Oh. I'm sorry. So, he's a sailor now? Do you see him much?"

"Once every couple o' years. That's why Father didn't want me looking for work in London the way Benny did, pro'bly getting myself in with a rough crew and whatnot. But I'm glad, wouldn't want to leave Mr. Sutherland."

"He does seem like an excellent person," Martha agreed.

"None better. Reasonable. Never comes the ugly and isn't afraid to get his hands dirty. Pays on time. Never promises the tenants what he can't deliver. True blue."

"High praise. I can see why you wouldn't want to leave Middlefinch."

"Aye. Which is not to say that the groom's quarters don't get a bit cold and lonely."

Martha bit her lip. Her two older sisters had warned her of moments like this. And as she'd reminded herself a moment ago, he was *not* actually her brother. He was handsome, too, but he did not greatly affect her heart.

Martha would probably not remain at Middlefinch all her life. She had no great desire to do so, though she liked Anne well enough. Also, Martha's mother had warned her that since John was marrying Georgiana, the younger three Turners—Martha, Ruthie, and Silas—would have to take care who they brought into the family. Martha was loath to appear proud and she was on the point of blurting out something apologetic when Timothy rubbed the back of his neck.

"You spend a lot of time with the mistress and... and Susan, eh? She's a lively girl, all right. Has she ever mentioned me?"

Martha felt a rush of relief. Unfortunately, she could not immediately think of an occasion when Susan had mentioned him. "Susan resents my position with Mrs. Sutherland," Martha explained slowly. "She would not confide in me. However, I should be surprised if she were indifferent to you."

They were back within sight of the house and the outbuildings.

James recalled that he was to check in with his bailiff and ordered Timothy to escort both ladies back to the stables and see them safely dismounted.

Anne was not sorry to see James go, but found herself a little lightheaded when she slid her feet out of the stirrups and Timothy helped her to the ground. Ever since they had crossed one of the fields which was newly sown with nitrate, the smell of which rather burned her delicate nose, her lungs had not felt right. The air seemed to become heavier and harder to suck in, and if she tried to take a large breath, it caused a tight ache in her throat.

"Martha," she panted. "I must go in at once."

It was going to be a bad attack; Anne could tell already. For instead of her breath easing, it only seemed to be growing worse. She tottered a few steps, but then Timothy scooped her up. "Pardon, ma'am. Allow me."

In the house, she did not trust Timothy on the stairs.

"James's study," she whispered. It was the most protected from drafts and from the coming and going of servants.

"Martha, fetch my powders," Anne wheezed, when he had set her down. "Perhaps they will help. Also, my vinaigrette and... and tell Susan."

Martha looked very much alarmed but dashed away and returned quickly. Susan was just behind her. Martha held a corked bottle of the Tunbridge waters.

"No," Anne coughed miserably. "Something hot." Sometimes the heat seemed to soothe her throat and unknot the tightness in her lungs. *An asthmatic fit,* the doctors called it. Suffocation was what it felt like.

Just then James entered. He looked surprised to see Anne, Martha, Timothy, and Susan. "Bailiff lost hope of me, I guess, wasn't to be found. What's to do?"

Anne began coughing again.

Martha gestured helplessly. "She has been wheezing since the stables."

"That won't do." James knelt and took one of Anne's hands, chafing it. "You looked so strong today, but damn if I didn't push you too far, lummox that I am."

Anne shook her head, but her paroxysm was growing markedly worse and James wanted to curse. He hated feeling helpless, and he hated being afraid. And was it his anxious imagination or were Anne's lips turning blue?

"Tea?" Susan gasped. "I have one of her powders here, but I do not think she can swallow it dry."

"Of course! Ring for it. Wait, no, John will be bringing me coffee any moment now. I generally have a cup with the bailiff... Timothy, go run to the kitchen and hurry him along."

He disappeared and James continued to rub Anne's hand. Despite the dreadful sound of her gasping, she did not look panicked precisely. Her eyes looked vacant, as if she had already given up. James would have preferred panic.

"Anne, do not worry, I will help you; you will be better directly. I'll send for the doctor—Good Lord, why have I not yet sent for a doctor?"

When John entered, along with Timothy and a tray of coffee things, James detached his hand from Anne. At some point she had begun gripping his.

He poured a cup of the stuff—it was very strong, the way he liked it—but poured in some milk to cool it for her. He dumped in one of her envelopes and also shook out a couple of the pills the Tunbridge fellow had drawn up for her. He put those in her hand as well, gently closing her fingers around them.

"There's a good girl. Let's see if this will help."

Anne choked and coughed but brought her little hand to her mouth and put several on her tongue.

James took a quick sip of the coffee to make sure it wouldn't scald her, and then put it to her lips. "Here you go. No, don't worry about spilling, just get a nice swallow or two." As he did so, he barked, "Timothy, go for the doctor."

Anne panted and coughed and tried in vain to clear her throat. Her cheeks were pale, but her neck and chest were flushed. She motioned and he brought the cup back up to her. This time she braced her hand on his to control it and managed to drink nearly half the cup.

"That's it," James said. "Nice and easy." He handed the cup back to Susan.

"I think she's getting easier, sir," Susan whispered.

"How can you tell?" James demanded. "She sounds ghastly."

But perhaps Susan was right, for though imperceptible from one moment to the next, Anne's color improved and her eyes became less dull.

She straightened herself a little and her breaths began to sound less labored.

"Perhaps a little more," Anne whispered.

James thankfully gave her back the cup and she drank it down.

Anne sagged against the chair. "I think that was the worst of it."

"More coffee?" James asked. "What else can I do?"

"No, thank you. Though it did seem to help faster than tea. I suppose just help me up to my room." She breathed in and out carefully. "I shall probably be exhausted for several days. I must be cautious not to get too cold or eat too much."

"What do you mean, 'cautious for several days'?" he demanded. "Do you mean that you have had these spasms before?"

Susan nodded. Anne looked confused. "Yes. At least several times a year. The last was in Tunbridge, so it has been a longer good spell than usual."

"But that's... that's monstrous. You were very ill."

"Yes," Anne repeated. "But you know that I am often ill, I told you."

James mopped his brow and pressed a hand over his eyes. "Sure and yes, you did. I suppose I thought I'd already seen the worst of it, however. It's not easy to sit back and see your wife nearly suffocate in her own phlegm."

Anne winced.

"Sorry, sorry. Shouldn't have said that. The truth is I'm right shaken." James levered himself unsteadily into the chair that was adjacent to Anne's before the fire.

He did not want to bury another wife.

23

OBIE CREPT PAST THE ROOM next to his. He did not want the alarmingly young, pretty girl who lived there to come out and say hullo. Whenever she caught him in the hall, he ended up giving her another story to read. It was quite out of his control.

"Good afternoon, Mr. Obie," she would say cheerfully. She had nearly black hair and large dark eyes and he always felt as if she was laughing at him. Maybe she was... maybe that was why she wanted to read his stories!

But she never laughed to his face. She would return a manuscript and smile brightly and sigh. "That was horridly morbid. I could not close my eyes all night, for thinking of that shrouded figure in the abandoned ruin! I do not know how you think of such things."

Obie would try to speak. Inaudibly.

"Do you have another?" she would ask prettily.

He would shake his head, but his traitorous lips were forming a *yes*.

"Wonderful!" she would clap her hands. "Just put it on the hall table there and I shall retrieve it tonight. Thank you! I adore your stories!"

And then... if he *did not* put one on the table, she might *knock* at his door and *ask* for it. At any time! He would not know when she might come.

That was dire.

He had to leave another manuscript on the table.

But this afternoon, the pretty girl did not seem to be in her room, and Obie was able to creep down the stairs without bother. Nor was anyone in the great hall or the front parlor where he could generally get tea with Beatrice and Mary. No, not Mary, *Anne*. He really must not allow his mind to be confused like that.

Beatrice and *Anne* were nice, comforting women. Elegant, of course, but not with that young, bright airiness that made him feel like a dried-up lemon rind.

But there was no tea. No fire either. He stuck his head in James' study—nice lad, James, always had been—but ducked back. They were all in there for some mysterious reason.

"Oh, Obie, it's alright," James said. "Have some coffee."

Well. That was alright. The study wasn't the place for tea, but if they weren't having tea, he supposed it didn't matter.

He came in gingerly and perched on the wooden bench beside the window. The pretty girl gave him some coffee but thankfully didn't talk to him. Looked rather pale, she did.

"You too, Mary," Obie said. "Pale."

"It's Anne," James snapped.

Anne put her hand on James's.

"Knew that." Obie said. He wished his words would come out of his mouth as easily as they came out of his pen, but alas. They did not. Though maybe the words should not come as easily as that last story had come. He felt a little funny about that one.

"She don't want to suffocate," Obie added, that being one of the interesting facts about Anne that stuck with him. Her pallor and strained breathing had reminded him.

She closed her eyes and took a long slow breath. "No, I certainly do not."

"Let's not talk about it," James said.

That was just as well. Obie needed to tell them something. "Need to go to London. Sign a paper."

"What?" James asked. "Do you mean another publishing contract? I thought you handled that through the post."

"Do. Can't. They wrote as I need to come myself."

"Well, we are going in March for the Season anyway. You can come up with us."

"Are you going to publish another story?" the pretty girl asked. "Do let me read it before you submit it to your agent!"

Obie shrank. "No. Already submitted it. Already published. Problematic." His eyes darted around. How to explain? The publisher had been vague, but Obie gathered there was definitely some problem with the book he'd submitted just before Christmas.

"Ah." Her face fell. "Of course, I shan't push you, then."

"I have more old ones," Obie found himself saying.

She brightened up. "Excellent. If you go up before I, just leave one on the hall table for me."

Obie sighed. Girls were tricksome creatures.

If, over the next few weeks, James did not play chess with Anne quite as much, or kiss her cheek when they retired, or hold her hand when she looked cold... he was not aware. His affection was at all times natural and uncalculated, and while that was in general a good thing, it also made him subject to the natural decline of emotion. While a more calculating person might simulate what they did not feel, at least for a time, to spare another's emotions, such wiles were beyond James. He was unaware of the change and thus unable to hide it.

The truth was, as they prepared to journey to London in mid-March—for Easter and the end of the parliamentary session when the men would be released from their duties and the real gaieties of the London Season would commence—James was instinctively protecting himself from pain.

Unfortunately, Anne did not know that. She had become a great observer of her husband, and his standoffishness was both noted and felt.

Exactly when had she come to find comfort from her husband's caresses? When had his hand on her back stopped being a noticeable and unwelcome strangeness and become a source of stability and contentment?

Anne spent the second to last afternoon at home sorting through her clothes with Susan, choosing what to bring to London and what to replace with new. She had never visited the London dress shops, milliners, glove-makers, and such things for herself. Her mother had always sent her measurements and orders to a London seamstress. Anne's clothes were always up to snuff, but she relished the idea of getting to peruse fabrics and patterns herself. To try on a multitude of hats before selecting one. To feel the weight of the shoes before purchase.

"This muslin is what... three years old?" she asked Susan. "You may keep that for yourself."

"Yes, ma'am, thank you." Susan put it on top of another dress that had been offered to her. It was expected that the castoffs of a lady went to her maid.

"Should I offer a few to Martha?" Anne pondered.

Susan huffed. "That would take some difficult alteration, ma'am. She being rather taller and broader than you."

Anne nodded. Did one even give castoffs to a companion? Anne had certainly never done so with Mrs. Jenkinson, but that lady was thirty years her senior and it would not have been appropriate. Lizzy had been around too short a time for the question to arise. Perhaps it would be as well for Anne to offer to buy a dress for Martha. One or two fine but plain dresses would do, so that Martha would not cause looks in London.

"But the expense." Anne sat abruptly. "All these clothes that I'm to replace, they will be quite a cost will they not?"

Susan was brushing off a pelisse that had acquired reddish dust at the hem. "I suppose the usual, ma'am."

"How much does a new dress cost? Why do I not know?"

Susan looked over her shoulder, perplexed. "It depends, does it not? Maybe ten pounds for one of these, but for a ball-gown... Lor', I don't know. Maybe fifty?"

Her eyes widened at the thought of such a sum, twice what she made in a year.

Anne frowned. She suspected Susan's guess was on the lower end of the spectrum. And how much did housing in London cost? And hosting a ball, which James continually assured her they should do. She wondered if Darcy had put it in the marriage settlements.

"Do the...do the servants talk about my husband?" Anne had never in her life *pumped* a servant; there had never been anything she deeply wanted to know.

"Well, there's talk and *talk*, if you know what I mean," Susan said. "Timothy has nothing but good to say of him. And Old Joseph don't hardly talk to anyone. Mrs. Gridley only tells us to mind our own business, though the serving maids... But I would *never* discuss my mistress or master, so her warnings are wasted on me."

Anne suspected from Susan's oddly emphatic tone that this was possibly not true, but that was not a rabbit trail to pursue at this exact moment. "You are not in trouble, Susan. I only wondered... do they talk about his finances? This London trip will be so costly."

Susan bit her lip. "There's always grumblers, aren't there? There's some as say he oughtn't to have done this or that—the new stove in the kitchen, belike, or some of his queer farming quirks—but they all like him, to be sure. I never heard that he was at *point non plus.*"

Anne was too uncomfortable to continue; Susan was starting to look at her rather oddly. It was most awkward when one realized that a servant was a person with their own thoughts and feelings. Really, it was information that must be suppressed, otherwise the sheer proximity of so many servants would leave one feeling quite exhausted.

Half-successfully pushing her new knowledge of Susan's humanity out of her head, Anne continued sorting. She put rather fewer items on the replacement list but was not foolish enough to think that a few dresses would make much difference.

James had assured her that he had a plan for the London expenses. That was good enough, wasn't it? It was not her responsibility to make all right. It was not her fault if James was in difficulty. For, although marrying her must have done great things with his creditors, her whole fortune did not automatically become his. Anne's dowry was invested, and she had far less than the thirty thousand pounds that had made Georgiana a notable heiress. The interest would be helpful but probably not make much difference for a man in James's position. Rosings Park and its environs would not earn him a penny in income while Lady Catherine lived.

But here she was doing sums in her head when she had just decided it was not her responsibility! Anne resolutely took herself away to be distracted in the

nursery, where Martha was no doubt playing with Barney. She sometimes did not know if James had hired a
companion        or        a        trial        governess.

{ 24 }

J AMES ATE DINNER IN A STATE of distraction, picking at his food, which was unlike him, for he was not a fastidious eater. His chef had already been shipped off to the newly rented London house along with several other key staff, so this meal was a step down, but it was not the food that was the problem.

At the table, which was now odd-numbered with the addition of Martha, Lady Beatrice covered a large yawn with her hand. "Do excuse me," she murmured. "I did not sleep well."

"Nor I," Obie agreed darkly. "London."

"Hm?" James said. They were to go on the morrow, and only James's knowledge that the journey was very short, hardly longer than it took to go to Rosings, convinced him to allow Anne to attempt it.

"Yes, I know," Lady Beatrice reassured Obie. "You do not like London. But you shall be with all of us, you know."

"Not at the publishing house." Obie dipped his head to slurp soup from his spoon. "Going alone. O. Finchley."

"Is that the publisher?" Lady Beatrice asked.

Obie tapped his chest. "It's me."

"Oh, that is your *nom de plume*? You never told me. Well, you will conduct your business and then we will send you home in the carriage and you will be comfortable again."

Anne was hardly eating anything, James noted. She had taken perhaps a teaspoon full of the jelly and a tiny piece of the fowl.

"Do you enjoy London, Lady Beatrice?" Anne asked. "I have never been. My mother does not prefer it."

"Why yes, for brief spells! I wouldn't want to be trapped there like a *cit*, but I'm happy to do the rounds for a fortnight or two. There's many as say they cannot abide the noise, particularly at night, but I do not find it too troublesome. Then there's the smell. That does cast a pall when one is used to the fresh air of Kent, but anything can be endured for a little, yes? I like taking rides in all the principal parks and seeing the new theater troupes and operas and so on."

"Do you attend the races?"

"Of course. The Ascot races are soon, and Epson Downs for Derby Day! Such grand times."

James sighed. Grand times they were, but grand times when his mother invariably gambled above her means. She was by no means always the loser, but that was to the worse. She had enough success to be always convinced more success was coming.

One could not blame her, however; it was in her blood. Her father had been an incorrigible gambler, and her brother too, James's late uncle. When gambling was in the blood, everyone knew there was no way to stop it. It was a mercy his mother was not addicted to cards. At least horse races were sporadic, and she could generally only attend the smaller ones held in their vicinity.

Still, he must have another talk with her about her limits. Perhaps with Anne to consider she would bring herself to remember his cautions when she placed her bets.

"I hope I may attend with you," Anne said. "I quite enjoy horse races."

"That's a capital idea," James agreed. When his mother went alone with Lord Nutley, she invariably shot the turf. "We'll all go; have a party of it."

Anne had not forgotten Darcy's words about Lady Beatrice and her gambling, but she could not quite picture James's mother in such activity. Was it not largely a gentleman's affair? Did Lady Beatrice stand in a great crush of gentlemen, calling out horse names and numbers and throwing her bonnet in the air when her choice crossed the finish line? Surely not.

Martha's eyes were wide, and Anne remembered that Martha's family probably considered gambling a sin. Martha did not drink wine, she did not dance, nor did she play games that involved dice or cards. Very severe, the Methodists were.

"You can still accompany me to such places, can you not?" Anne asked her. "Even if you do not quite approve of the activities?"

Martha nodded vigorously. "Of course, ma'am. Though I am always happy to stay with Master Barney when you don't need me."

Lady Beatrice shook her head. "I still don't know but that you should leave him here, James. London is no place for children."

James sipped his wine. "I don't like to leave him alone in this great place for so long."

"It's commonly done," Lady Beatrice said. "I did not bring you to London until you were old enough for Oxford."

James didn't express reproach, but his words were blunt. "Yes, I know. Very lonely, I found it. I shall enjoy taking Barney to see the sights. The Royal Menagerie, the Bond Street bazaar, Regent's Park... he will love it."

Anne felt a stirring of interest herself. She was not so much interested in lions and bears, that was a childish fascination, wasn't it? But... still, it would be a shame not to see such sights when she had the opportunity.

"The house we let is just north of Green Park," James added, "where Nurse and Barney may go for walks. And the house is next to a courtyard where Barney may play ball or romp about with the other children of the neighborhood."

"I don't suppose..." Anne faltered. "Perhaps it would have been better to accept Darcy's offer to use their town house again? Is it too late to change the accommodations?"

"Yes, much too late. And besides, I told you I should do everything shipshape and Bristol fashion. When we arrive, you must begin seeing about the ball we shall throw. Find out what type of refreshments and musicians are in vogue and so on. That's all you need concern yourself with."

Perhaps James meant to be reassuring, but his abrupt answer made Anne feel inexplicably left out.

"As you wish," she said.

Martha took Timothy's hand to hop down from the carriage when they arrived at the London house, but she had no eyes for him.

"Look at this place!" she whispered. She put a hand over her nose as well. London truly did stink, though not quite as badly here as some of the neighborhoods they'd driven through.

"I've seen many like it," he said loftily. "M'father may not have wanted me to find work here in London, but he brought me with him on occasion."

"This does not impress you at all?" Martha waved her hand at the grand houses in a row, impressive façades of rich gray or yellow stone, white columns, and shiny, cut-glass windows that twinkled and illuminated the light from within like the pieces of a chandelier.

He shrugged. "All very fine, I suppose. Not to compare with Middlefinch."

Martha snorted. "I don't believe you. You sound like Silas when he wouldn't admit he was impressed with Pemberley."

Timothy's mouth tweaked upward, but now Martha saw that Anne was out of the carriage and... and Mr. Sutherland was *not* offering his arm as he always did. Instead, Susan stood at Anne's side as Mr. Sutherland walked with his mother.

Had Anne and Mr. Sutherland quarreled?

Martha's concern for her employers eclipsed her first view of the house, which left a jumbled impression of colorful wallpaper, claw-footed settees, and pseudo-Egyptian art. Wouldn't Ruthie stare to see it?

The house was four stories tall and only a few rooms wide, which meant that Martha's room was perforce on the top floor with the other servants. There was no ballroom, exactly, but a large salon on the third level, which would be cleared of furniture for the party they would host.

Martha tagged along half-heartedly as Susan and Anne entered her new room. Anne was never what one might call a chatterbox, so it was difficult to tell if her quiet was merely weariness, or if James's unusual slight had affected her. It was acceptable for Mr. Sutherland to escort his mother... but it would have been just as acceptable to leave Lady Beatrice in the comfortable hands of Bronson, the butler, or even Obie. It would have been thoughtful to escort his wife when he first brought her to their temporary new home.

"I shall lie down," Anne said. "Susan, wake me for dinner. Martha, tomorrow we must discuss getting you a few serviceable gowns for London, when you accompany me on morning calls and such."

Martha and Susan quietly slipped out, and Martha couldn't help but notice the very irritated look on Susan's face.

"Is something the matter?"

Susan sniffed. "Nothing at all, miss. Excuse me."

But Martha's room was also on the fourth floor, so they walked together up the stairs. "What is it, Susan?"

Martha finally demanded. "I have three sisters and three brothers, you know, I can tell when someone resents me. Is it that I am Anne's companion? I daresay it's only temporary."

"I'm sure I do not care."

"Is it the dresses? But you always look so nice! Your clothes are better than mine," Martha added truthfully.

"Of course they are. They are from my mistress."

"Then..."

"I daresay she will get you a fine new riding habit as well. I never learnt to ride sidesaddle like a lady."

Martha frowned. "Did you very much want to? I don't particularly care for it. It's most uncomfortable. And when Timothy throws me up, I feel as if I shall tumble off the other side... Oh."

For Susan was looking quite fierce and silent again. She turned into her room, which she would share with one of the housemaids, and kicked the door shut with her heel.

Martha placed her small valise in her own room, a smile growing. She did love a good romance, and here she was in the middle of one! London and a romance to boot. How her life had changed in the last six months!

Martha went to find Barney and Nurse. Barney was pressed against the window which looked down at the courtyard. "May we go for a walk, Martha? Please?"

"I should like it," Martha agreed. "Then Nurse may have a moment to get your things settled in the nursery.

They descended back through the house with a delightful feeling of adventure. Just inside the front door was a side table with a mound of letters and calling cards on it.

"Good gracious," Martha exclaimed. "Mrs. Sutherland must have a wider acquaintance than I knew."

But Barney did not care about this mystery. He and Martha hurried down to cut behind the house and enter the green space he'd spied from his window.

Martha directed Barney past the carriage house, a small building tucked behind the row of houses, where they found Timothy polishing the mud-splattered box of their carriage.

"Going to the park?" he asked. "Probably oughtn't wander off alone. Need company?"

"I didn't grow up in the country," Martha retorted. "I may not have been to London but I daresay I've seen more of the manufacturing districts of the north than you."

"London ways are different," he said with simple confidence.

"Indisputably, but I see three children out there with none but a nursemaid, and so I am unafraid."

Timothy nodded, taking her retort in good humor.

"I just had a most interesting conversation," Martha said instead. "With Susan. I imagine she will want to see a few sights on her half day off."

"Eh, what's that?" Timothy perked up, tossing his rag from one hand to the other.

"Maybe you should offer to accompany her."

OBIE CLUTCHED HIS OWN LETTER in his hand, and when Martha and Barney were safely away, he waved down a hackney. He carefully repeated the address to the man, "34 Deresham Street, in the city."

It was just past five in the afternoon and starting to get dark. The gas lanterns along the road were not yet lit. Obie was not certain if this was an appropriate time to conduct business, but this *was* why he had come to London. The sooner his business was complete, the sooner he could go back to his peaceful rooms at Middlefinch. All the more peaceful if the family stayed away for a few months.

Obie did *not* want to be in London when James and Anne had their fancy party. They would expect him to *come*. Possibly to *speak*.

No, no. 34 Deresham. Deresham 34. He was nearly there when it occurred to him that he could have gotten Timothy to take him in their own carriage, but it was too late for that.

"Here you go, sir," the hackney driver said.

The cobblestones were more worn and cracked here. Between them was a kind of sludge that made Obie step carefully and wrinkle his nose.

The modest front door had a sign that read, "Mason & Mason." Reassured, since Mr. Robert Mason was his correspondent, Obie entered.

There was a fireplace in the small anteroom, but it had burned down to all but ashes and Obie looked around apologetically. "Too late," he muttered to the empty room.

A lamp on the side table provided a little yellow light, but he did not hear any voices or movement from the room beyond. He leant against the wall by the door and fingered the folded letter in his hand uncertainly. He did not know entirely what it meant—he had never been good at reading between the lines—but the phrases "unexpected notoriety" and "delicate matter" filled him with uneasiness.

Just then, the inner office opened. A middle-aged gentleman went to the lamp and snuffed it.

Obie straightened. "Excuse me."

The man spun with a hand on his chest. "Goodness, sir, you blended right into the wall. Excuse *me*, how do you do?"

"I do," Obie said, shaking his hand. "Blend in with walls."

"I was just closing up. How can I help you, Mr....?"

Obie blinked. Of course. Mr. Mason did not know who he was, they had only corresponded. He held up the letter. "I am Obadiah Sutherland," he explained. "Family calls me Obie."

"You—You're—"

The man looked perplexed. Obie held out the letter. "O. Finchley, that's the name I use."

"Of course. Only...I expected..."

Obie was not always the most perceptive, but he deemed that the man was rather more surprised than he ought to be. "Something wrong?" Obie asked. "Asked me to come in, didn't you?"

"Yes, quite! Forgive me. You told me you lived with your nephew in Kent, I just... to be honest, since you always signed your letters O. Sutherland, I thought the initial was perhaps for Olivia or Ophelia or Octavia..."

"Those are female names," Obie said, puzzled.

"Yes, it was stupid of me... Your writing is such that... never mind!" He opened up his office, which was cold but made Obie feel more at home. "I must congratulate you, sir. While your previous stories have sold decently, particularly to the lending libraries—that is why we haven't asked you to front the cost since the first volume—the latest one has become all the rage! Do sit, please," he interjected, dusting a perfectly clean seat with his handkerchief. "We shall do a third printing of it as soon as possible, and perhaps another printing of your last volume, now that you are *known*. The *beau monde*—the nobles and highest families, you know—quite eat up the gothic and macabre, and this latest story about the automaton has captured their collective imagination."

Limply, Obie sat.

"Beyond the lending libraries, the *beau monde* are the major purchaser of books," Mason continued, "and their patronage equals success."

Mason's desk was neat and tidy, but he tidied it even more before unlocking a desk drawer and retrieving a veritable mountain of correspondence. "Now, first, I must tell you that we at times receive letters directed to the author. A fad no doubt, but you have received so much in the past two months, I thought it best to give it to you in person. Saves the postage.

Obie took the pile of mail. "For me?" he said. "I never receive letters from anyone except you."

"Well, you do now, sir. I shall begin forwarding all correspondence. Now, the real reason I asked you to visit, was...ahem... personal." He cleared his throat a couple times. "You see, somehow it has become known that O. Finchley is a member of the Sutherland household. We at Mason and Mason would never divulge information entrusted to us, but the fact is... somehow it has become known."

Obie put the letters on the chair next to him. "They know it's me? I never intended... I do not much like meeting strangers or interacting. But no one knows the Sutherlands..."

"I'm afraid it's worse than that." The man shifted uncomfortably. "I must also explain that books whose characters are closely based on real people are also the rage just now. Which means that, at the moment, every book is read with an eye toward identifying the genesis of the characters. Your automaton, Mary, has garnered much interest."

Obie began to feel a little sick.

"Your latest book, well, people have decided the automaton is Lady Catherine's daughter, the one Lady Catherine always claimed would marry a certain Mr. Darcy."

"But... Anne is not famous," Obie objected. "Never been to London. Told me so."

Mason inclined his head. "Unfortunately, Mr. Darcy *is* well-known. Pemberley is in all the guidebooks, you know, sir. And there was a bit of talk when he married to disoblige his family. As for Lady Catherine, although she has not come to town for some years, she is still well-known. She and her husband were quite active in society twenty years ago, and she seems to be related to everybody of note. In short, people knew *of* the new Mrs. Sutherland, and the very fact of her rather reclusive life only leant color to the story. The automaton who murders her husband, she is based off Mrs. Anne Sutherland, yes?"

Obie took out the stub of a pencil in his pocket and tumbled it 'round in his fingers. "Maybe just... She helped me with the idea, you see. And perhaps just her appearance... her mannerisms...."

The publisher grimaced. "Yes, I was afraid of that. She may need to be prepared that... she is something of a sensation just now."

Obie accidentally flicked the pencil onto the rug. He stooped his aged body to pick it up. "Have I caused a scandal?"

"Perhaps not quite that bad... but, talk, sir, a good deal of talk."

"Oh, dear." Obie chewed his stub of a pencil. "Poor Anne. Poor James. Didn't ought to have written it."

Mr. Mason, his questionable news delivered, was growing more cheerful. "We have deposited your advances and royalties into an account at Hoare's Bank, as you instructed, save for the twenty pounds per annum you have always received."

"Is there much more than that?" Obie asked.

"Well, not to put too fine a point on it, but yes, sir. Hoare's would like your signature and address on file; I assume you will visit them while you are in town."

"I have to go to a bank, too?" Obie asked, nonplussed.

"I shall be happy to escort you myself. Shall we say, tomorrow at noon?"

"At the bank?"

"Yes, sir." Mr. Mason now seemed to be measuring Obie's responses. "You may make a large withdrawal while you are there. It is your money, after all."

Obie shook his head. "Don't need any more. Still have ten pounds in my drawer at home."

"Whatever you think best. Just know that if you need any money for personal, family, or other reasons, you have upwards of two hundred pounds in your account. It will probably soon be doubled."

Obie blinked. He was not good with money, never had been.

"Also, I have a copy of the book for you," Mr. Mason said happily. "We had it bound for you. And if you wish to have your copy illustrated, I can give you several recommendations."

He fished a slim, handsome, burgundy-colored book from another drawer. "Our compliments, sir."

Obie took it, but his hands were shaking. It *was* undeniably exciting to have his very own book in his hands. If only it had been in other circumstances!

*A Gentle Touch; Or The Automaton Who Made Tea*
*By O. Finchley*

And on the title page: *In which a man's sanity is destroyed as he falls in love with his wife, a life-like automaton with murderous propensities.*

Obie groaned. "I should not have written it."

After a discreet silence, Mason cleared his throat. "Might I see you home, sir? London can be a bit intimidating at night, for those not used to it."

"I can't," Obie said. "Ashamed. Idiot."

Mr. Mason cocked his head. "Perhaps a drink? Calm your nerves? There's a snug little pub around the corner."

{ 26 }

ANNE DRESSED CAREFULLY BEFORE the evening meal, striving to overcome her drowsiness. For their first meal in the new townhouse, James had invited Lizzy and Darcy as well as Lady Honoria and her husband to join them for an early supper. An early supper for London, that is. Eight in the evening seemed late enough; Lady Catherine abhorred town hours and Anne found she agreed.

It would not have been Anne's choice to have guests so soon, but then James had not been inquiring into her preferences of late. Anne heard him dressing in his own room, directing a word or two to his man. Then James's heavy footsteps retreated down the stairs. He did not offer to walk down with her. He did not even poke his head in to see how she liked the new house.

Anne sighed at her own silliness. She placed a lace mantilla over her wine-colored gown and knocked on

Martha's door. Anne did not expect a very enjoyable evening.

To her surprise, however, when Anne faced Lizzy, it was the cozy night in Martha's bedroom awaiting a baby that came to mind, and the quiet evening they'd spent playing chess. Those memories had almost completely overwritten the aggravation of their first months of acquaintance. Anne felt a little surge of energy, rather than annoyance.

She embraced Lizzy and smiled a little quizzically. "I suppose I *am* glad to see you."

Lizzy laughed. "Why, thank you. If we are being honest, I find I am not sorry to see you either."

Lady Honoria also greeted Anne as a friend of long standing, and what's more, it felt true. Anne did not find Lizzy's laugh so loud and annoying as it had once been. Perhaps Lizzy had finally acquired some refinement. Or perhaps Anne had grown less exacting.

Both ladies also greeted Martha warmly. How odd to think that Martha would soon be Lizzy and Darcy's sister! The thought amused Anne instead of horrifying her.

The gentleman grouped themselves at the other end of the long drawing room, exchanging pleasantries and enjoying a dry white wine before the meal.

"Allow me to introduce you to Lady Beatrice," Anne said.

Lady Beatrice greeted Lizzy and Honoria, but she kept looking distractedly toward the stairs. "Martha, have you seen Obie? One of these new London servants says he went out almost as soon as we arrived."

"He is not in the house?"

"No."

"Obie?" Lady Honoria asked.

Lady Beatrice nodded. "Mr. Obadiah Sutherland, my uncle."

"The mysterious O!" Lady Honoria exclaimed. Then she grimaced expressively. "Do excuse me. But it has been such a rumor and we weren't certain..." She exchanged a look with Lizzy.

Lizzy also grimaced, but with a twinkle in her eye. "I feel we must explain immediately, but I hope you will both choose to be diverted and not angry. Honoria, perhaps you should do the honors. I myself have only just arrived in London and have not even read it yet; I only know what I have heard from you."

"Read what?" Anne asked. "One of Obie's stories?"

Lady Honoria interlocked her fingers uneasily. "His last story, which I gather that he wrote quite recently, has made a huge hit. Everyone who is *anyone* has read it—sorry, Lizzy, you are behind—and the prevailing notion is that the main characters are based on you and James."

Lady Beatrice raised a brow. "But no one reads Obie's stories, do they? I know we paid for the first printing..."

"Perhaps, ma'am, but this one has been read. I believe the presence of the Sutherland family in town this season is... hotly anticipated."

As if on cue, a loud and persistent knocking was heard from the front door.



Bronson, the Sutherland's butler, did not care for London townhouses, or London ways. The knocker had not yet been placed on the front door, as the family was not yet 'at home' to callers. Only bad taste would cause someone to ignore that socially accepted signal and bang on the door with their fist.

When the miscreant knocked again, Bronson descended the stairs in irritation. He opened the door with his sternest expression. "The family is not—"

But it was Mr. Obadiah on the step, a slightly tipsy Mr. Obadiah, escorted home by a businessman.

"Ah, good evening," Mr. Mason said, introducing himself. To do him justice, he had not realized how little alcohol his new author friend was accustomed to. He nudged Obie upright, for he seemed predisposed to sit on the stoop. "That's right, Mr. Sutherland. Home now, in you go."

The butler grasped Obie's elbow to steady his staggering step.

Mr. Mason handed Bronson a pile of correspondence and a book. "These are also his. Thank you! G'night!"

Bemused, Bronson set those on the table next to the *other* stack of letters and grabbed Obie before he could sit down again. He knew better than to escort Mr. Obadiah into the drawing room with the family and guests, particularly in his current state. Bronson encouraged him to shuffle discreetly up the stairs. Later Bronson would drop an unobtrusive word in Lady Beatrice's ear so she would not worry.

But on the third floor, Lady Beatrice herself suddenly flung open the drawing room door and stopped him. "Is that Obie?" she demanded. "Bring him in here, Bronson."

"My lady, he is not... fit to join company at present."

"Nonsense. I know he is not dressed, but we have several pressing questions for him."

"Lady Beatrice—"

"Obie, come in at once."

Obie burst into tears.

"Oh, gracious heavens."

"My lady," Bronson said. "I believe he has...er, had a drop."

Lady Beatrice looked chagrined. "I suppose we will get nothing out of him now. This confirms my fears."

"If you allow me, Lady Beatrice, I believe some coffee and food would do him good."

Obie wiped his eyes and unearthed his handkerchief to blow his nose. "Messed up. Idiot."

Lady Beatrice returned to the drawing room. "I am afraid it is too true," she told Anne. "He has just come in and...is the picture of guilt."

Anne dropped rather ungracefully onto the settee. "I cannot believe it. How could he put me in a novel? It is degrading."

Lizzy put her arm around Anne. "It is a shock, I do not deny, but not *degrading*. Many consider it an honor to get even a *mention* in one of these society books, and you are the central character! I should live to be so lucky."

Anne felt a withering reply form itself, but Lady Honoria jumped in.

"Lizzy!" she chastised. "I know you love fun, but this is truly a blow for Anne. As an unknown member of the *ton*, as a newly married lady, as Lady Catherine's daughter... this is serious."

"How notorious am I?" Anne asked Lady Honoria. "Shall I have to go back to Middlefinch?"

"No, on no account. The story is outrageous and fantastical. You only need show yourself a woman of breeding and good-humor and intelligence. It will soon be forgotten."

Martha turned for the door. "I shall get her vinaigrette."

The gentlemen had finally realized something was amiss, and James, Darcy, and Chuff broke off their conversation about the war and joined them.

Darcy put his hand on Lizzy's shoulder and she rested her hand on it. James only looked quizzically at Anne.

Chuff shook his head at Lady Honoria. "You told her? I warned you, you should wait. May turn out to be nothing."

"Have you read it, also?" Anne asked, too mortified to be timid.

"Ah. Well, yes, Honoria told me to. Dashed good yarn, if a little verbose."

Lady Beatrice quietly informed James of the circumstances.

"A murderous automaton?" he repeated incredulously.

Chuff nodded. "The automaton suffocates her husband, and... Well, chills ran down my spine, don't you know? Then she places a crown on his head—for he had been teaching her chess, you see—and we realize she has mistaken the lessons for real life. When she discovers he will not reset for a new game, the springs, gaskets, and pneumatic tubes that make up her brain begin to lock up. She sits down by the fire and becomes as still as a rock, hands curved like claws on the arms of the chair, repeating, 'Illegal move. Checkmate.' The servants find them both dead."

Anne and James stared at him. Lady Honoria stood and smacked him. "You did not have to blurt out the most gruesome part, dear. The poor girl is already in shock."

{ 27 }

THE DINNER WENT FORWARD despite the cannon-ade that had been fired into their ranks, but James could not say that anyone made a hearty meal of it, except perhaps Chuff.

James speared a grape on his fork. "Whatever that book may say, no one can say for certain that Obie based it off Anne. It must be pure speculation."

Lady Honoria looked as if she wished to agree with this, but honesty forbade it. "The description of Mary is exactly Anne, and the circumstances are regrettably similar. No one meets Mary until her marriage, on account of "chronic illness," and she was—forgive me, Darcy—engaged to a high-ranking gentleman who reneged at the last moment in favor of a lively commoner. There is even some sort of scandal attaching to the lively commoner's sister."

"Good god," Lizzy said. "If Lydia ever learns that she has been novelized, there will be no living with her."

Darcy frowned at her and Lizzy shrugged apologetically. "Yes, I know it is awful, but repeating that *ad nauseam* does no one any good. The thing that I cannot fathom is who made the connection? Your uncle's pen-name, O. Finchley, is perfectly common. Who knows the Sutherlands well enough to have made such an intuitive leap?"

James speared another fruit savagely. "Surely we can scotch the book? I know it has been published, but if it is libel...? Obie will retract the whole if we ask."

"I fear that would only add to the scandal," Lady Honoria advised. "I think—if it could be managed—that the best course would be to proudly own the whole. To express pride that Obadiah is an accomplished novelist. To laugh at the similarities but not deny them. To remark on his droll ability to sketch a character...that sort of thing."

"Lady Jane!" Martha announced triumphantly.

The assembled company looked at her, and Martha colored with embarrassment. "I do beg your pardon. It just occurred to me that Anne told Lady Jane and I the rough idea of the story—the automaton and the suffocation—at Pemberley. She might have made the connection."

Lady Honoria knit her brow. "That seems entirely likely."

"But it does not matter who started the rumor," Anne said wearily. "If it is known, it is known."

James shook his head. Even if he could boldly face down such scandal, he did not think Anne could brazen through a whole London Season in such a way. Lizzy or Honoria might have done it, but Anne?

"How many copies were published?" James asked. "Do we know? I still think our best option is retraction."

Lady Beatrice pulled the bell rope. When the butler appeared, she rose. "Bronson, it is time to fetch Obie for us. Bring him to the drawing room; I think we have all eaten as much as we can."

By the time they assembled in the drawing room, which was on the floor above the dining room, Bronson had realized that the infamous book in question had been unceremoniously thrust into his hands earlier.

"If this will be of use, sir..." He tactfully passed it on to James as they entered the drawing room.

"What? Lord, we have a copy already? Thank you, Bronson."

James tucked it away under his jacket and joined the others.

Obie was looking chastened and a little red around the eyes. He also looked deeply unhappy to be placed in the center of such a group.

Lizzy and Honoria were whispering to their husbands.

Darcy nodded immediately. "We don't wish to intrude on family business. You've only to send me a line if there's aught I can do, but for now we'll take our leave."

Honoria and Chuff followed suit, leaving only the family party.

"Now, Obie," Lady Beatrice said, rather less gently than she usually spoke to him. "What have you done?"

"Wrote a story," he said miserably. "Anne's idea. The automaton, the suffocation, and the chess. Very *good* ideas."

"But how has there even been time?" Lady Beatrice demanded.

"Story came easy. Wrote it quick. Mason says they contracted with several printing houses to get the copies done in January."

"But how did you... why did you describe me so clearly that people would notice?" Anne asked.

"Didn't mean to. Just...happened. You sat so still. Stared at nothing. Didn't laugh."

Anne cringed. Was her behavior so life-less? That hurt her almost as much as the rest. "I do laugh."

"Not often. Don't draw. Don't play. Don't sew. Blank."

The strange looks on James and Beatrice's face told their own tale. Was this how they all thought of her?

Only Martha defended her. "What are you speaking of? Anne is not *blank*. She writes letters and spends time with Barney every day that she can. She likes fashion and cats and chess. When it is warm, she rides, and she cannot wait to begin going regularly. She even likes listening to Obie's stories. She enjoys selecting gifts months in advance... I already know what she has for Lady Beatrice's birthday! Anne is *not* blank."

Obie stuttered an apology mixed with a truthful protest that he *liked* Anne's quietness, but it was James's and Beatrice's stunned faces which Anne watched. James rubbed his mouth and seemed to avoid making eye contact with her.

After a prolonged pause, Lady Beatrice pulled herself together. "That will do, Martha. We must focus on the issue at hand. Obie, how many of your books were published?"

"Mason says an initial run of a hundred. Second run of four."

James rocked back on his heels. "Five hundred books? I'd thought maybe eighty or ninety..."

Obie's concave chest seemed to sink in even more. "Can I go? Need to lie down."

"Why not?" James waved a hand and sank into a chair while Obie disappeared. "The issue at hand then, is what to do next. Anne... I think the decision must be yours. We cannot undo what has been done. Do we stay to face down the *ton,* or do we retreat to Middlefinch and plan for next year? I am sure such a farce as this will be forgotten by then."

Lady Beatrice's mouth fell open. "Retreat? But you have already let the house. I have made plans with several particular friends! I counted on being here at least until late mid-May. We cannot leave now."

"Mother, I appreciate all that, but it must be Anne's choice. She is the one who has been wronged the most."

"I understand that. Though, honestly, I do not think Obie is so much at fault. If one will sit in front of the fire for hours at a time—"

"Mother!"

She relapsed into silence.

Anne rose. "I do not think I can decide tonight; I am overwhelmed. Please excuse me."

In his room, James took off his necktie and waistcoat and threw them on the bed. He didn't know when he had been in such a taking. Everything was a mess.

And it wasn't just this business with Obie, though that was a rare tangle. It was that somehow, in the course of things, it had become Martha who saw Anne more clearly than her own family.

He sat down and slid off his shoes. Martha, who had only known Anne for three months! But maybe that was *why* she saw more clearly; she saw only who Anne was now. No history.

Blast it all.

James went to the connecting door which led from the master's room to the adjoining one. "Anne? May I come in?"

There was a pause. "Yes."

Anne was wrapped in her dressing gown. The bed was mussed as if she had lain down but then gotten up when he knocked.

"I'm sorry," James said. "I thought you were still up."

"It's fine."

"No, nothing is fine. We started off well, but this last month I feel as if we've become strangers again." James led her to the divan which was wide enough for the two of them. Sitting, he held one of her hands in his lap.

"This is not about Obie's book?" she asked, confused.

"I don't rightly know. It is and it isn't." Her hand seemed softer than it had been, less bony. "I think it's my fault. I was so focused on making you well, that when you had that attack in February—I couldn't take it. Felt I'd failed you. Felt I'd lose you the same way I lost Milly."

"But... you have not failed me." Anne's hand moved a little within his. "I am much better this winter than normal. No, truly," she shushed him, "although I have ill days, I *must* be healthier, for I shake them off almost at once. Even that asthmatic fit did not lay me out for more than a day."

"But I wanted more. I want you to be completely well!"

Anne laughed softly. "You sound like Barney."

"Do I? I feel like him, too. I may soon throw myself on the floor and yell if I do not get my way."

Anne patted his shoulder. "I would like to be well, and I hope you will keep trying—as long as you do not fixate on anything too disgusting. But I also think, as Martha would probably say, that we cannot demand health from the hand of Providence. Perhaps I will continue to get stronger, perhaps I will stay as I am now, perhaps I will sicken and...and die. None of that will be your doing."

"That does not feel true."

"But it is."

They sat thus for several minutes.

"Am I so lifeless that I seem like a machine?" Anne asked presently.

"No!" James shifted so that he could pull Anne into his lap.

She yelped. "This cannot be proper."

"It isn't," James said. "And you are not lifeless at all. I am sorry that Martha was the one to say it, and not I. You are much more than that. I will admit that when you are not feeling well, you tend to disappear into your own thoughts, but now I know what it means. You are not lifeless, Anne."

Her rigid posture slowly relaxed. "I'm glad. I don't want to be." She looked at him a touch severely. "Mind you, I don't want to be a Lizzy Bennet, either."

James laughed and hugged her. "I wouldn't want you to be her. Besides, I like to talk far too much to be married to such a lady as that. I am happy with my Anne, who listens to me as no one else will, and even remembers what I say!"

Anne smiled, but then tensed up again. James tightened his arms, not ready to end their time together.

"There is still the matter of the book," she said. "And whether to go or stay."

"Whatever you wish."

"Would it be... helpful if we delayed until next year?"

"Helpful?"

"Financially. I wish you will tell me how... how badly we are in debt. I would wish to be helpful, or at least to make wise choices, but I do not know how concerned to be. For instance, since your mother bought that horse—"

"Golden Breeze," James supplied.

"Yes, Golden Breeze, I do not know how that impacted you or your spending this year. I do not know if you can get the money back on this house—would that be a loss?—or if it would be easier to incur the expense of a season next year. I do not even know how much a ball gown costs."

This last comment, almost petulant, made James laugh. "Nor do I, for that matter. Ought we to call for Bronson and ask him? I am sure he knows." Anne made to get off his lap, and he held up his hands. "I jest. The truth is that nine hundred pounds, though extremely ill-advised, did not hurt me overly. She once lost four thousand in a day at Ascot."

"Four thousand *pounds*?"

"Exactly. So, would this season put me in further debt? No, at least in so far as dresses and furbelows and hats go. If you also have gambling tendencies however, then we should probably leave London at once."

"I don't think I do. I like races, and I like picking the winner, but I have no great desire to put a fortune on it."

"Smart girl."

"Can you not...stop your mother?"

He shifted, absently rubbing her back. "That is a tricky thing, isn't it? I could spread the word that none of her bets will be honored, but that is considered an extremely nasty thing to do. I have attempted to remonstrate with her, and she perfectly understands... until she stands at a racetrack again, perfectly sure which ones will place. I could forbid her visiting London, but that seems churlish and hard-fisted for a son to do to his mother."

"That is a dilemma," Anne admitted. She yawned.

"I should let you rest. I apologize again for what Obie has done. You may take your time deciding how to respond."

He scooted Anne to the seat next to him and leaned over to kiss her goodnight. Instead of aiming for her cheek, he kissed her on the mouth. "Sweet dreams."

{ 28 }

ANNE DECIDED THAT THEY WOULD stay in London. They were here. All the plans had been made. The work was done. Surely she could hold her head high for a few weeks until the interest in Obie's book died down.

Her first task was to go through the mountain of mail that had been delivered to her. Anne read them and dictated her replies to Martha.

"No one dares come out and say I am the murderess in a novel. It is only, 'as an old friend of your mother, I am delighted to invite you to my daughter's musical soiree,' or, 'as an old friend of the Darcy family, I hope you will accompany us to the theater on Thursday next,' and so on."

"Perhaps that is truly what they mean," Martha offered.

"I do not think I have heard of the half of them, and I am sure they have not heard of me. It must be that wretched book."

On the positive side of the scale, Anne had so many invitations that she could quite fill her calendar with pleasant things. Whether the *company* would be pleasant remained to be seen.

Many invitations had to be rejected, which Martha also carefully penned, "With sincerest regrets, Anne Sutherland," or "With deepest apologies, Anne Sutherland."

"I do not know that I am apologizing," Anne protested.

"It sounds grand though, does it not? You must be above any gossip."

"I suppose."

The second task was to read *the book.* James almost did not allow her, but Anne insisted that she must know the worst in order to be prepared for unexpected comments.

"It is necessary," Anne argued. "If I am to play this off in a proud way, I must be able to say I've read it."

James sighed and gave her the slim volume. "Just remember that it is all ridiculous."

It *was* ridiculous. If Obie had not hit off the characters in such a detailed, life-like way by copying her and James, it would probably not have been so engrossing.

She wondered if his previous works were as good, or whether she had offered such inspiration as to raise his art to a new level. She supposed there was some comfort in that thought.

Where Obie himself excelled was in the atmospheric details. The delicate but cold ceramic of the lady's fingertips. A rat running over a pale foot. The sound of grinding pins and beating pistons instead of a heartbeat. Sleeping next to a mannequin with eyes wide open. The mounting dread of the husband's nightmares.

Thankfully, by the time the automaton actually murdered the husband and broke down, Anne had grown more comfortable. The characters diverged so far from her and James at that point, the likeness did not bother her.

"I have finished." Anne returned the book to James.

The first test of her mettle was at a small party that evening. It was an invitation from Lady Honoria, who could be trusted to set a congenial tone for the gathering.

Anne and James arrived in their carriage at nine, and a footman handed them down. Anne was wearing one of her favorite evening gowns. Fawn lace fell gracefully over a green underskirt, with a simple beaded bodice.

"I say," James said as they walked up the steps, "we never discussed how we should behave to one another at these events."

"How do you mean?"

"It would probably be good if we were viewed as too affectionate, rather than the opposite."

"Oh. Yes, I see."

They did not have time to discuss it further, as they were escorted up to the party.

Lady Honoria greeted them at once, warmly taking Anne's hands. "Good girl, you look quite the thing, without being at all pushing."

She introduced Anne to several ladies, but it was a casual party, so there was little formality. Conversation was the order of the evening, and the guests were free to arrange themselves how they liked and speak to whom they wished.

Anne found herself at the center of a knot of ladies rather rapidly.

With another quick clasp, Lady Honoria broached the subject at once. "Anne has recently introduced me to her uncle, the author. Such an unusual man, so droll."

Anne followed her lead. "Yes, but he won't stay in London long, I fear. He much prefers the country."

The lady next to Anne leaned forward. "I have just been reading his latest, *A Gentle Touch.* It is chilling, is it not?"

"Quite!" Anne forced a laugh, but she was afraid it sounded mechanical and made a mental note not to do it again. "His descriptions are uncanny. But I found the whole premise rather ridiculous. He does not even discuss where the creature came from."

"That is true..."

Another lady chimed in, "My sister and I quite adored it. There is a real automaton at the British Museum which plays the pianoforte! You must see it while you are in town. Perhaps you could play a duet!"

"That sounds delightful." Anne felt bold. "But I do not even play the piano myself, so you see I should make a poor automaton."

A startled laugh followed this.


Lady Honoria almost gaped. Where had mild-mannered, placid Anne de Bourgh gone? She watched in satisfaction as Anne circled throughout the evening making new acquaintances. Not all her replies were as clever as that first sally, but she held her own. She was not always conciliating, not always laughing, but she would pass anywhere as a woman of sense and dry humor. What's more, she carried herself like a married lady of several years' experience, with quiet confidence.

James took her into supper, which was rather odd since normally couples did not partner with one another. It was not enough to set tongues wagging, but it was enough for people to say that they were unbecomingly besotted with each other, which was all for the best.

After supper, Anne settled into an armchair.

"You are doing splendidly," Honoria said. "Are you quite exhausted?"

"Yes, to be frank. When is it appropriate to leave?"

Honoria was glad that Anne didn't stand on such ceremony with her as to be afraid of giving offense with such a question. "You must stay for tea, but soon thereafter you may complain of London hours and go home."

Another passel of young ladies came up then, led by a Miss Donnel, who had a quantity of golden ringlets and eyes set rather far apart. "Lady Honoria, will you introduce us to your friend?"

She did so and the young ladies sat on the pretty Chippendale chairs around Anne.

"I hope you do not mind my saying so, but you are quite how I pictured Mary! It is most diverting. Do tell me what it is like being in a gruesome novel." This was rather bold, even for Miss Donnel.

Anne pursed her lips. "To be sure, it is amusing, but it was a rather uncomplimentary portrayal. Imagine if you were portrayed as a pretty, but empty-headed doll, for instance." Anne's voice was not cruel, but several other girls chuckled.

Miss Donnel shook her curls. "I'm sure I shouldn't mind."

"Then that is very good-tempered of you," Anne said, relenting, "and speaks to your better nature. I am afraid I felt rather churlish about the whole thing."

Lady Honoria moved away again, confident that Anne would do well. She had a biting tongue, it turned out, but seemed to be kinder than her mother.

{ 29 }

IT WAS ONLY A FEW DAYS LATER, when Anne and Martha were returning home from a mantua-maker, that Lady Catherine's unexpected arrival shocked the Sutherland household into disarray.

Her trunks and bandboxes were stacked against the wall in the entryway, which was the first warning Anne had. Bronson attended them at once, removing the boxes from Martha's hands and communicating imperturbably, "Your mother has come, ma'am. She is in the drawing room awaiting your return."

"She...she has come to stay with us?" Anne asked.

"I do not know. I offered to immediately move her things to a guest room, but she declined."

"How strange."

Anne mounted the stairs slowly, wondering what brought Lady Catherine to London. She made no secret of disliking it. But since she had come, why would she not stay with them?

"Mother," Anne greeted. "How wonderful to see you so unexpectedly."

Lady Catherine bumped her jaw against Anne's cheek in a sort of kiss. "Yes, my dear. I am here. I notice you didn't invite me."

"I—did not think you would want to come." Anne seated herself. "Allow me to introduce my new companion, Martha."

Martha curtseyed and Lady Catherine harrumphed. "She's pretty. Too pretty. I made that mistake with Lizzy, so you'd best be rid of her before she makes off with your husband."

Martha sat, eyes wide.

Anne's mouth fell open. "Mother. That is beyond the line, surely. Let us talk of your stay. Bronson says you did not allow him to take up your things. We have two guest rooms; would you like to select which one you prefer?"

"I do not know that I am staying."

"Ah. Perhaps you will stay with Darcy and...and Lizzy?"

Lady Catherine snorted. "Not likely. I should prefer a hotel."

"Ah." Anne waited. "May I ask how Charlotte and Baby Catherine find themselves?"

"Fine, they are both fine. Aren't you going to offer me tea?"

"Of course. Martha, see to it."

Lady Catherine looked up and down the drawing room. "I suppose you know why I've come."

"No, Mother. Though I am glad to see you, of course."

"Did you think no one would tell me? It is this *book* nonsense."

Anne exhaled. "Oh, I do see. Thank you for coming, but you need not worry. James and I have decided to remain and put the talk to rest. I do not know what exactly you were told—"

"Everything." Lady Catherine thumped her cane as she was wont to do when angered. "I read the horrid thing myself, being sent a copy by one of my old friends. That idiot uncle slandered you and your so-called husband. He implied more than a little about the Darcy family; he even slandered *me.*"

"Did he?" Anne thought back. She supposed there were a few background passages that implied Lady Catherine had deceived James in order to get him to marry Anne (or Mary), and that Lady Catherine had lied to the world about Anne's illness in order to prevent the discovery of her foul nature.

"He most certainly did. And what I want to know is what's being done about it. That a scandal should attach itself to our family in this way is quite infuriating. That business with Lizzy's little trollop of a sister was bad enough. And I cannot even *discuss* Georgiana without becoming overwrought, and at my age that cannot be healthy, so do not tempt me. But *you...* I had thought that you were safe from scandal. You have never been the sort of girl to cause the least anxiety—at least, anxiety over anything other than your unending illnesses—and I cannot and *will not* tolerate you and I being subject to public speculation." Lady Catherine sucked in a breath. "We will leave at once. You will not even return to Middlefinch to face further insult, for we will send for your things. My only question is whether you can leave today or if you will need until tomorrow?"

Anne wet her dry lips. "I do not perfectly understand. You want me to return to Rosings? To leave James?"

"Nothing of that sort, though I cannot like that man. He is disrespectful and mocking. I do not doubt that he knew all along about that abominable book and allowed it!"

"He did not. Even if he did... my leaving him would cause a far greater scandal than some silly book. Is it not a scandal that we are trying to avoid?"

"I am not suggesting divorce, for heaven's sake. No one will look askance at a long visit to your mother. That dratted uncle, the author, lives at Middlefinch and you cannot continue on with him. Clearly you need guidance. I suggest the man be packed off to Bedlam."

Anne nodded slowly, though she had no intention of punishing Obie. She was beginning to understand. Her mother loved to be useful, to give advice, to straighten up any crooked matter. She also prided herself on the heritage, dignity, and prestige of her immediate and extended family. And during one tumultuous year, she had lost nearly everything.

Darcy, the prize she had long claimed on Anne's behalf, was snatched away. The prestige of arranging a good marriage for Georgiana was destroyed. Her familial pride was besmirched by Lydia Bennet's attempted elopement and sudden marriage. And now this book cut at the dignity of herself and her only daughter... it had been too much.

What exactly James had done to incur Lady Catherine's displeasure, Anne was unsure, but it was no doubt related.

"Mother, I am not going to leave James, not even temporarily. That is out of the question. But if you stay in town a few days, I think you'll find that the rumors are already abating. In fact, your presence would be excellent, for it will further prove the ridiculous nature of the book."

Lady Catherine must have known that her request was on the borderline of unacceptable, for she accepted

Anne's rebuff with better grace than expected. "I don't like it. I don't like any of it."

"Nor did I," Anne agreed whole-heartedly. "I was very angry, in fact."

"Hmph."

"Obie has already been packed off to Middlefinch alone," she added. It was true, though Obie had all but *begged* to be excused back to his home and they had all agreed that he would do no good trying to join society.

"Indeed."

"We go to the theater tonight and to Ascot for the races tomorrow. You might enjoy it. Lady Beatrice will attend, as well as her friend, Lord Nutley."

"Nutley? He dangled after me the first year I was out, although he was much too young. Your father called him a silly cub. The man hasn't changed much."

Anne blinked, struggling to think of the rotund, middle-aged Lord Nutley as a silly cub. "Indeed, you must have many more acquaintances here than I do. Will you stay?"

"I suppose I shall have to. I won't have the last vestiges of our family pride drug through the mud by the London gossips. Yes, very well. Tell that chit Martha to make herself useful and find my maid. She's probably off gabbing with the London servants. Everyone knows they have lazy ways. And *where* is the tea?"

{ 30 }

ANNE HEARD JAMES COME IN much later from the lecture he'd attended and hustle up the stairs to change. If she had to guess, he'd probably remained behind to ask the lecturer about breeding sheep that didn't bleat or some such craziness.

Anne knocked on his door for the first time. "James? Could I speak with you before we go down?"

He opened the door at once. "Are you feeling ill? What's the matter?"

"No. My mother has come for a visit," Anne explained at once. "I did not realize; she did not write... But, of course, I convinced her to stay. She will be down for supper momentarily."

James whistled. "Ah. Well, that's capital, of course. Happy to have her. Didn't think she'd come."

Anne was silent. She felt one instinct to apologize for her mother's presence and the unpleasantness that was sure to occur, and an opposing instinct to defend her mother. It was not as if James's mother was perfect, after all! But that seemed unnecessarily combative and would require a longer explanation.

"She is unhappy about the book," Anne said. "And that aggravation has spilled over to other things. I hope she will not be harsh with you."

James chucked Anne's chin gently. "Well, and if she is, I shall not blame it on you. We will be fine no matter what she says, yes?"

"Yes," Anne said. "Th-thank you."

James was about to turn away—he truly did need to change, or else Lady Catherine would find his lateness another reason to be aggravated—but Anne was looking at him oddly.

"Yes, Anne? Something else?"

"You...you are rather an excellent person. Did you know?"

James chuckled. "Trying to turn me up sweet?"

"No. I am lucky—blessed—to have gotten such an excellent husband. You are better than other men," she finished simply.

"Not at all sure *that's* true..."

"It is." She hesitated, then squeezed his hand. "I'll meet you downstairs."

James felt positively light-hearted at dinner, despite the cloud that hung over Lady Catherine. She found room for improvement in everything.

From the soup course, "I shall have to give your cook my recipe for pickled garlic, it makes all the difference," all the way to dessert, "This lemon cream is tolerable—you brought the lemons from your own lemongerie, you say?—but how are they stored, that is the question? I really must inspect the pantry and see if they are far from the stove. Citrus is so vulnerable to heat. I made them reorganize the entire larder at Blenheim, you know."

Lady Beatrice disagreed with most of Lady Catherine's remarks, but at this one only smiled tightly. "That must have been a Herculean task. We quite trust our cook and housekeeper, however."

"You can never truly trust a servant," Lady Catherine objected. "My abigail has been with me nigh on thirty years, and I still check my jewels when she has gone."

"What an uncomfortable way to live," Lady Beatrice said.

"Coffee or tea?" Anne interrupted. "Before we go to the theater."


When they left the table, Anne put her hand on Lady Beatrice's arm. "Stay a moment."

"Yes?" Lady Beatrice asked.

"I know my mother can be...opinionated, but she does not act on every suggestion she makes. It is just her way."

"You might need to remind her that it is your house," Lady Beatrice said.

"I might. In the meantime, may I suggest that a gentle touch will do?"

Lady Beatrice's full mouth flattened out. "Yes. I know I told you so about Obie, but he truly *is* harmless. That is... I had no way of knowing that *Mary* was the name of a homicidal character..."

"No, of course not. But as my mother has not yet caused any *serious* trouble to our household, I think she deserves as much consideration." Anne continued on to the parlor. "I have never been to a play; I am quite excited."

It was true that the play would have been more enjoyable without her mother's occasional comments on the staging and direction, but it was still a memorable evening. Not least of which was the amount of notice Lady Catherine received from the other patrons. She would always have had acquaintance in London, she being young enough that many of her generation were still to be found mingling at every posh event, but the book had reminded everyone of who she was. Friends and acquaintances came out of the figurative woodwork to make themselves known.

If Lady Catherine rankled at a few too-freely-made comments about her daughter's unexpected notoriety, thankfully the crush of people visiting their box prevented more than three or four sharp retorts. Her biting comments about fictional fairy tales were met with enjoyment, and people only said that they well remembered Lady Catherine's blunt sayings.

All in all, Anne felt that it went excessively well. What's more, she experienced a strange sort of kinship with James throughout it all. They were hardly by each other's side, but all it took was a lifted eyebrow or half-smile for them to share the experience with the other. It was like having a partner, or being on a team, perhaps. Maybe what having a close sibling would have been, but even better.

Anne was exhausted when they arrived home at one in the morning, but when James stuck his head in to say good night, Anne smiled sleepily from the bed. "Wait. I meant to ask what lecture kept you late today?"

He laughed and rubbed his eyes. "It was a talk on elemental identification. Sir Humphry Davy has now identified five more elements. Calcium, magnesium, boron, chlorine...I forget the last."

"Does that...help with farming?"

"No, not at present." James perched on the side of her bed. "I stayed behind to speak with him about schooling. In about five years, maybe less, Martha's young brother

Silas will be ready to attend one of the universities. I was in favor of Oxford, but after explaining the circumstances to Sir Humphrey, he suggested New College in Manchester. There's a great scientist there, Dalton, who teaches. He's a Quaker, from a humble background, and Silas might do well with him."

"But do you think Silas's parents can afford to send him to even a small university? I suppose they managed with John..." Here was yet another cost Anne did not know.

"Well, don't forget, my dear, that John is marrying Georgiana in a month."

Anne covered her mouth against a yawn. "I forgot again; how silly of me. They can easily send him to school."

"Exactly. What he'll need, however, are connections, and I thought I might be some help in that line. Maybe in a year or two I'll take him to meet this Dalton. Eager chap, Silas. Liked him." Now James yawned. "Neither of us can keep our eyes open. We are country people. Good night, my dear."

{ 31 }

THE ROYAL ASCOT RACES were everything Anne could have wanted. This was the last day of the four-day event, the only races held at Ascot, and it seemed all of London had turned out.

Today the horses would compete for the golden cup. The Royal Enclosure was nearby, but only those invited by the royal family could sit in those stands. Anne was content to stand in the fine places James procured for them.

She loved the smell of the turf and the horses, though the smell of the common people she could do without. She also loved the way the horses flew down the brown tracks, looking as if they had been shot as bows from an arrow.

Lady Catherine and Lady Beatrice stood nearby with Lord Nutley.

James leaned and spoke in Anne's ear. "That is an interesting development. I'm curious how it will work out."

Lord Nutley was dividing his attention between the two ladies, but they were not making it easy. Both of them were accustomed to command in their own circle.

Lady Beatrice waved over to the paddocks. "I see they are walking the contenders, but I cannot see from here. Do let us walk over and examine them."

"Quite." Lord Nutley was all agreement.

"The ground is quite soft here. I cannot imagine why they do not make platforms for the gentry. If I should be on the committee, I should insist upon it," Lady Catherine animadverted. "Give me your arm, Nutley. I shall accompany you."

The whole party trailed after them. Anne was also curious to see the horses from as close as the spectators could get. A few of the horses were merely grazing in makeshift pens, but most were being led about by grooms, slowly warming up for the race and acclimatizing to the presence of the large crowds.

"That one," Lady Beatrice said, "fourth from the left with a blaze? Fine straight hocks. Large chest. Sloping shoulders."

"A little too large in the chest, I should say," Lady Catherine said. "Don't like his action."

Lady Beatrice frowned. "His forward action is superb. Which do you prefer?"

"Don't know all at once, do I?" Lady Catherine retorted. She watched for some minutes. "I'll put my money on that chestnut, he's not overfleshed. Got a smooth, strong gait to him."

"Ah, your ladyship wishes to wager?" Lord Nutley asked.

"Just said so, didn't I? Going a bit deaf, are you, Nutley?"

"No, no."

"Well, get over to that betting stand for me then, and put ten guineas down."

"T-ten guineas?" the poor man stuttered.

"You are getting deaf. You'll need an earhorn soon."

James turned a laugh into a cough. He whispered to Anne, for in the press of people it was easy to be discreet. "He's accustomed to much bigger commissions. To see your mother sending him like an errand boy for ten guineas... it makes me quite vindictively happy."

"Only ten guineas?" Lady Beatrice said. "Are you not certain of your horse, Lady Catherine?"

"How could I be, after only a few minutes watching them? Now my husband, Sir Richard de Bourgh, he would research the history, the races, the sires... he knew his business, he did. Even then he never bet more than ten pounds. Do it for pride, not money, that's what he said. Money cheapens it."

Lady Beatrice sniffed. "A most unusual sentiment. I still prefer the blazed black. I didn't want to puff of my knowledge, but as a matter of fact, his name is By-Your-Leave, and his sire is Golden Breeze, who now graces our stables at Middlefinch. He's a winner if I have ever seen one. He took the silver at Epsom Downs in the three-year-old race."

"Hm. Well, put your money down and we'll see, won't we?" Lady Catherine said.

Lady Beatrice looked between the two horses.

"Never bet out of sentimentality," Lady Catherine added blandly. "Sir Richard also said that."

Lady Beatrice all but snapped. "Did he have any other maxims?"

"Several, but I won't trouble you." Lady Catherine looked as pleased as a cat with cream.

Lady Beatrice nodded and glanced at James and back at Lady Catherine. "In that case, Lord Nutley, I believe I will wager..." She softly named an amount.

"Speak up!" Lady Catherine demanded. "He's deaf as a post. Won't get it right."

Lady Beatrice glared. "No need, Lady Catherine—"

Lord Nutley looked very unhappy. "Unfortunately, didn't hear you. Crush of people, you know."

Lady Beatrice smiled tightly. "Fine. Ten guineas on By-Your-Leave. For pride."

Lady Catherine nodded. "Anne, you may choose one as well. I'll spot you the ten if you need it."

This unexpected inclusion pleased Anne. "Thank you, Mother, but I'm sure James will 'spot me' what I need.

"Happy to," he replied at once. "Which horse shall we wager on?"

"We?" Anne asked.

"Of course. I want to wager ten guineas myself, if that's how the play is going today."

Lord Nutley sighed.

Anne pondered the horses. "The blaze and the chestnut are both very fine, probably the best here."

Both Lady Catherine and Lady Beatrice looked at her sharply. It was as if a sudden test of loyalty had arrived.

His mother or her mother?

"I think... I should like to put ten on Sir Archibald's roan," Anne said, pointing.

Lord Nutley cleared his throat. "The young lady may not be aware that he was a last-minute entry. The original horse entered by Sir Archibald sprained his fetlock only a fortnight ago. This 'un barely meets the requirements. Even Sir Archibald is not betting on him."

"I had heard that," Anne commented. "Sir Archibald was at the theater complaining of the situation. And I am not wagering that he'll win the golden cup. I'm putting ten on him for third place."

"As am I, then," James said. "Twenty on Sir Archibald's roan for third."

Lady Beatrice wrinkled her nose. "I wouldn't criticize for the world, but that is a strange choice. Almost any other horse has a better chance."

Lady Catherine was for once united with Lady Beatrice in abusing this decision. "Capricious, Anne."

"For horse racing is such a weighty matter," Anne said.

Lady Catherine looked at her narrowly, unable to tell whether Anne was jesting or not.

When Lord Nutley returned from his humble task, they turned back toward the carriages. Lord Nutley offered his arm to Lady Beatrice, whom he had squired here, and James offered his arms to Anne and Lady Catherine. Passing by the Royal Enclosure, Lady Catherine sniffed audibly. "As one would hope," she said ineffably.

James had planned to borrow a high-perch phaeton, but that would have been extremely difficult for Lady Catherine to climb into. Instead, he'd rented an open carriage for the occasion, so that they might sit at their leisure and look down on the race. Lord Nutley had a low-perch phaeton, which was situated next to theirs.

Lady Catherine raised a hand to further shade her eyes, which were already quite protected by the audacious hat she had worn for the occasion, purple with feathers. "Anne. Why *did* you bet on that roan? I thought you were a better judge of a horse than that. Feeling obstinate?"

"No. Or perhaps yes. I like the idea that he may *place*, though I know he will not win. It is always better to play the game than not."

Lady Catherine would have shaken her head if not for the hat. "You shouldn't say such things to other people, they don't know you as I do. They'll think you're philosophical."

An hour later, Lady Beatrice looked at Anne with new respect. "I cannot believe the roan placed third." She was in a caressing temper, for her own pick had come out first, and so she was perfectly ready to heap praise on Anne as well.

Lady Catherine's choice had come in second, but in criticizing the decision of the jockey to go for the inside—which had clearly lost him the finish—she was almost as satisfied as if he had won.

Lady Catherine reached up with her cane and poked Lord Nutley. "You'll have to descend again into the fray to visit the betting stand. Otherwise some blackleg may disappear with Anne and Beatrice's winnings."

"Not at the Royal Ascot," he protested. "The betting men will stand by their word. I usually settle things over a pint in the morning when it's all calmed down."

"No time like the present," Lady Catherine insisted.

James took pity on Lord Nutley and patted Anne's knee. "I'll just nip down and settle then. I think we did rather well. What were the odds? Seven against? I'll return in a moment."

Lady Beatrice fanned herself. "Dear James is always so considerate. I must say, I am satisfied with this win, despite wagering so little."

Lady Catherine shifted to face the other carriage more easily. "Lady Beatrice, perhaps I'll join you at the Lingfield races in June. You generally enter one of your own horses there, do you not?"

"Yes, that is correct. I have a very promising three-year-old. High hopes of him."

"Then we shall have a rematch. I still hold that the chestnut could have won if properly ridden."

"Blood will out," Lady Beatrice argued.

"Until Lingfield, then," Lady Catherine promised. "You must bring Anne as well; it will be a treat for her."

Anne smiled. Although condescending, her mother was attempting to do something pleasant. "I should like that very much," Anne said. "And you must come to Middlefinch for Christmas. I am thinking of having our own house party this year..."

# Epilogue – Four Years Later

ANNE RECLINED ON THE LOUNGE in her room at Middlefinch, pained and exhausted, but happy. It was spring again, and the orchard that was visible from her window was pink with blossoms. They were cherry trees, with some apricot and plums, but mainly cherry. The roses along the walkway were budding, with an occasional early rose, though not many.

Anne's cat, Poppy, was sprawled across the coverlet on the bed, warming herself in the mid-day sun. Anne's new maid, a girl they'd hired recently, after Susan had married Timothy, was righting the bed covers.

Nurse brought Anne a whimpering Humphrey, only two days old, and Anne held him wonderingly. She had never thought she would have such a perfect son. It seemed rather incredible to her, and she lived with the niggling fear that he would inherit some of her predisposition to illness. James prevented her dwelling on it most of the time.

So far, Humphrey was a healthy, if fussy infant. He had just been fed and cleaned and was inclined to be sleepy but could not seem to go to sleep without crying. James had hired a wet-nurse so that Anne could rest and recover after the delivery, which she was devoutly thankful for. She swayed back and forth, hoping the motion would help him close his eyes.

There was a light tap on the door and Nurse opened it.

"Is this the right time?" Barney asked.

"Yes, just past noon," Anne said. "You're on the mark." Barney entered softly with Martha, who was now his governess. Barney was a hearty eight-year-old and far into the learning of Latin declensions and grammatical diagrams necessary for Eton.

"Humphrey," Martha cooed, capably taking him in her arms. "Ah, he is a fine boy. Silas will love his name, by the by. He adores Sir Humphry Davy."

Barney's lips twisted from side to side. "A brother. I do wish he would grow up fast enough to play with."

"He will," Nurse scolded, "but you're not to go carrying him off to see a bird's nest, hear? Or putting him on a pony without asking us. Plenty of time for that when he's older."

Barney sighed. "I know. Can I at least hold him? I feel I have a right to that, don't I?"

James looked in from the next room. "Doesn't work quite like that, but I think you may hold him if you are careful."

Martha leaned the wrapped baby against Barney's shoulder and made sure his hands were in the right places.

Barney patted Humphrey's back and beamed. "I am good at this."

Nurse snorted. "Don't be getting above yourself—"

The baby belched loudly and Barney froze. "That wasn't me."

James laughed. "We know. It was your manner-less little brother here. You will have to teach him how to behave like a gentleman."

Nurse soon shooed them all from the room, except James, who was the only one who could shoo *her*.

"I shall be back for Humphrey in twenty minutes," she said firmly.

James rocked the baby while Anne stretched. "It's like the first time," he said. "Perhaps fellows who have twelve children grow used to it, but I certainly have not."

"Perhaps my mother will be reconciled to staying at Middlefinch now that we have a son."

"What do you mean? She's already reconciled to it," James said. "She comes and tell me what to do with my tenants and crops and cattle...she is perfectly reconciled."

"But she's unhappy when we don't do it."

"In a way, but there is part of her that enjoys the challenge. That way when I *do* follow her advice on something, it is a real triumph. She has not stopped crowing about the wet nurse."

"And the beets."

"Exactly. Intermittent victory is all the sweeter. That is why she and my mother have become racing cronies, no doubt. They both enjoy beating the other more than anything else. I am devoutly thankful, for I should have hated to take racing away from my mother. I wasn't sure it would last, but somehow your mother has shamed her out of high stakes in a way I never could."

The baby gave another belch, and finally seemed to grow weary of struggling. His head drooped against James's arm. "Look at him. Already lifting his head at two days. He's a strong one."

James handed the baby back to Anne. "You are strong, too, Anne. I love you very much."

"And I love you."

Lady Catherine opened the door. "I have just seen Barney, who says Humphrey is in here. If you will be guided by me, you will allow my grandson to grow accustomed to sleeping in the nursery. It is best to begin as you mean to continue."

"Very well," Anne said with a smile. "I will allow Nurse to take Humphrey in a few minutes."

Lady Catherine nodded decisively. "And then you must rest. I know as well as anyone how exhausted you must feel."

Humphrey gave out one last, loud wail before subsiding into a doze.

Lady Catherine tapped her cane with satisfaction. "I always said that if Anne could have children, she would bear fine, strong sons."

*The End.*

# Author's Note

THANK YOU FOR READING *An Austen Ensemble!* This was my first foray into regency fiction, and for a lover of Jane Austen and Georgette Heyer, that was intimidating.

In this last story I leaned more into the mystery and medical side of things. I gave Anne high functioning autism, COPD, and anemia. Thankfully, the waters of Tunbridge Wells are high in iron and other minerals, and would have helped her. James was certainly ahead of his time, but there were about to be big strides taken in medicine, so he is only a *little* precipitate. For example, Sir Humphry Davy, whom they name the baby after, was already identifying new elements, making batteries, and experimenting with laughing gas for surgeries at this time. In my head, Silas Turner is going to be one of those ground-breaking scientists. With patronage from the Darcys and the Sutherlands, he will be able to devote most of his time to experimentation. He and Barney remain friends until they are old men.

Thanks again for reading and don't forget to check out my other books and series!
Corrie Garret

The Highbury Variation
*From Highbury with Love*
*From London with Loyalty*
*From Pemberley with Luck*

Pride and Persuasion
*Starch and Strategy*

Modern Retellings
*Pride and Prejudice and Passports*
*The Rise and Fall of Jane*

Find more at corriegarrett.com
Or on Facebook, at Corrie Garrett, Author

www.ingramcontent.com/pod-product-compliance
Lightning Source LLC
Chambersburg PA
CBHW061220310726
48971CB00007B/1880